ghost, interrupted

By Sonia Singh

GHOST, INTERRUPTED
BOLLYWOOD CONFIDENTIAL
GODDESS FOR HIRE

ghost, interrupted

SONIA SINGH

AVON
TRADE

An Imprint of HarperCollinsPublishers

GHOST, INTERRUPTED. Copyright © 2007 by Sonia Singh. All rights reserved. Printed in the United States of America. No part of this book may be used or reproduced in any manner whatsoever without written permission except in the case of brief quotations embodied in critical articles and reviews. For information address HarperCollins Publishers, 10 East 53rd Street, New York, NY 10022.

HarperCollins books may be purchased for educational, business, or sales promotional use. For information please write: Special Markets Department, HarperCollins Publishers, 10 East 53rd Street, New York, NY 10022.

FIRST EDITION

Interior text designed by Diahann Sturge

Library of Congress Cataloging-in-Publication Data

Singh, Sonia.
    Ghost, interrupted / by Sonia Singh.—1st ed.
        p. cm.
    ISBN: 978-0-06-089022-3
    ISBN-10: 0-06-089022-3
    1. Parapsychologists—Fiction. 2. San Francisco (Calif.)—Fiction.   I. Title.

PS3619.I5745G47 2007
813'.6—dc22   2006021566

07 08 09 10 11 JTC/RRD 10 9 8 7 6 5 4 3 2 1

For my brother, Samir,
who spent countless hours
critiquing the chapters in this book.
I know, I know,
I should have come to you sooner.
P.S. Sorry about the double vision.

My thanks to:

Kimberly Whalen, for buying me drinks and for being cool with my neurotic, insecure, mood-swinging, over-eating, genre-changing self.

Lyssa Keusch, who didn't bat an eye when I followed a chick-lit novel about Bollywood with a comedic novel about ghost hunting.

Avon Books, for giving me the best book covers in the business.

Lucinda Ferguson and Shelly DeSimone, the critique goddesses.

From Ghosts and Ghoulies
and Long-legged Beasties and
Things that go BUMP in the Night,
May the Good Lord Deliver Us!

—Old Cornish prayer

Your house may be haunted

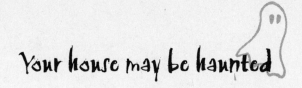

If you find your head spinning uncontrollably in a clockwise direction or a counterclockwise direction. The direction really doesn't matter.

If you ask a question in an empty room and the room answers you.

If unseen forces move your furniture around, particularly in the direction of your head.

If your child comes to you one day and informs you that the TV is the conduit to another dimension inhabited by the spirits of people buried under the house, and the spirits really want to play.

If the exterminator tells you that the knocking in your wall isn't caused by rats but by an ancient Babylonian demon named Mazuzu.

If a priest, a rabbi, and a nun aren't the beginning of a joke, but a list of visitors you've had over recently.

Disclaimer
The views expressed in the list above are solely those of the individual providing them and do not reflect the opinions of The Cold Spot: Paranormal Investigations, its parent, affiliate, or subsidiary companies.

1

Anjali

San Jose, California

When Anjali was a kid her parents made her promise never to tell anyone she was psychic.

Personally, she'd found such a precaution unnecessary but she swore anyway.

Honestly, did her parents think she'd go around making introductions like, "Hi, my name is Anjali Kumar and I can communicate with the dead. What's your name?"

That's right.

Anjali could communicate with the dead, but she couldn't beat the house in Vegas.

Go figure.

She was the black sheep in the family, the skeleton in the closet (although thanks to a certain fondness for vodka and chocolate, she hardly considered herself bone-thin).

But Anjali wasn't in the psychiatrist's office that gloomy afternoon to talk about her parents . . . much.

She was there to talk about the whole psychic thing. Or rather, a way to shut it off.

Namely drugs.

If Prozac could quiet a child's love of starting fires, then surely it could help her—a woman too psychic to function.

Across the cherrywood desk, Dr. Feldman held court in a plush leather armchair. The smile she leveled carried a distinctly patronizing glint. "You realize, Anjali, that everyone is born with some extrasensory ability. Knowing the phone is going to ring before it does. Disliking someone you just met without knowing why . . . but reading minds, communing with spirits . . . well, that just doesn't exist. All of the world's so-called psychics have proven to be frauds."

Great.

How could Dr. Feldman—a psychiatrist who bore an eerie resemblance to Barbra Streisand—possibly help her when she didn't believe psychic abilities were real? When she didn't believe Anjali's problems were real?

Anjali wished she'd never made the appointment. She'd gotten her hopes up after seeing an ad on TV. The actress in the commercial with the soothing voice had promised, "Whatever your problem, a little white pill can help."

Whatever her problem . . .

After she hit puberty, Anjali's abilities had zoomed into warp drive. She had only to touch an object to know who held it last. Any wonder she wasn't a big fan of vintage clothing?

Anjali had no clue where her so-called gift came from. According to what she'd read, a person was usually born with ESP, inherited through DNA like blue eyes or male pattern baldness. At twenty-eight she had the same golden skin, brown eyes, and wavy black hair as the rest of her family. But to her knowledge, none of the other Kumars ever slapped a bumper sticker on a car that read: *Honk if you're telepathic.*

Sometimes Anjali wished she was just plain old crazy.

There was nothing wrong with crazy. They had a cure for crazy. Crazy was good.

Sanity was overrated.

Dr. Feldman steepled her hands and narrowed her eyes, focusing on her patient. "Now Anjali, this problem you have of being overly sensitive to the world around you—"

Translation: *Another neurotic basket case.*

"—merely nerves. A change of scene might be in order."

I co-own a sanitarium.

"There are methods of relaxation you can try—"

Electroshock therapy is making a comeback.

Great. Of all the luck, she'd managed to find the one psychiatrist in the nation who didn't leap at the chance to prescribe medication. And Dr. Feldman was the only shrink in the area she could afford. Her crappy-ass health insurance didn't cover psychiatric consultations.

She'd tried everything and every form of therapy to gain control of and subdue her ability: yoga, transcendental meditation, regular meditation, therapeutic art classes, rebirthing, past life regression, interpretive dancing, and sensory deprivation. Nothing worked.

"Let's get back to high school," the good doctor delved. "You'd begun describing those years to me."

The words slipped from her lips before she could stop them. "They called me Carrie."

"Carrie?"

"You know the movie with Sissy Spacek? Pig's blood on prom night?"

"And how did that make you feel?"

Lame question alert!

"Angry, of course . . . but eventually the teasing stopped."

"Oh?"

"Well, I reminded them of what happened at the end of the movie. Carrie mentally locked the doors of the gym and everyone inside was burned alive."

"Aha." Dr. Feldman began scribbling something in her notepad.

Anjali took a deep breath. She had to give this one more shot. "Dr. Feldman, I really think what I need is an anti-depressant or maybe a tranquilizer? Just something to dull my senses, help me get through the day?"

"Tell me more about wanting to kill your classmates," the doctor prompted.

Anjali dug her nails into her palms and bit back a scream of frustration. Dr. Feldman was no Barbra Streisand and this wasn't *The Prince of Tides*. She'd get no help with her demons.

She took a deep breath and tried to center herself. After all, it could've been worse. Dr. Feldman could have pre-scribed what countless relatives had—a husband. Time and time again she'd heard, "You're a pretty girl but you're nearly thirty—*Hai Ram!*—and your looks won't last forever."

Oh, who was she kidding? There was no antidepressant on earth that could shut down her sixth sense.

Unlike most people's image of a psychic, Anjali Kumar did not have gruesome dreams of serial killers committing their crimes, nor did she make millions dispensing advice via a 1-900 number.

Being psychic was not as cool as it sounded.

2

Scott

San Francisco

"Are you on welfare?"

In the middle of adjusting the optical zoom on his digital camcorder, Scott looked up to see a chubby, freckle-faced, ginger-haired boy of about eight or nine hovering in the doorway of the guest bedroom. "Sorry?" he asked.

The boy entered the room and went straight for Scott's camera. "Granddad says anyone who isn't at work during the day is a bum on welfare." He pressed his fingers against the LCD screen and began twisting the lens.

Scott gently removed the boy's hands from his expensive equipment and tried not to grimace at how sticky the fingers were. "Cody . . . right? Your grandmother asked me to check out the strange noises she's been hearing in the walls."

Cody stuck one of his sticky fingers into a nostril and began digging. "That doesn't sound like a real job."

Scott shuddered and looked away from Cody's nasal excavation. "Now you sound like my father."

When Scott informed his family he was quitting his job as stockbroker to pursue his passion full-time, his father, Garrison Wilder II, had been somewhere between infuriated and deranged. Garrison refused to tell his friends and colleagues that his namesake, Garrison "Scott" Wilder III, was now a full-fledged ghost hunter.

Scott's response was to inform his father that his correct title was paranormal investigator. The term *ghost hunter* conjured up an image of a sunburned, straw-haired Australian, dressed in khaki shirt, matching shorts, and brown boots, stomping through a haunted house shouting, "Crikey! Ghosts rule!"

Scott's father failed to see the difference.

Scott's mother was a bit more understanding. She'd been the one to tuck her young son in bed at night, gently stroking his brow and removing the book he'd fallen asleep reading. Books with titles like *Decapitated Spirits: The Ghosts of Windsor Castle* and *Violent Deaths: Why Ghosts Demand Revenge*.

Meanwhile, Scott's younger brother, Ethan, was off skiing in Zermatt with his fiancée and could not be reached for comment.

At thirty-four, Scott looked like a typical Wilder male. He possessed the classic Wilder attributes: dark hair, dark eyes, strong white teeth, height, and a shrewd financial instinct. From what he'd learned, none of his predecessors, however, had ever possessed the slightest interest in the paranormal.

"Spookology," his father called it.

"Granddad says people who don't work are degenerates and drug addicts," Cody said, reaching for the camera again.

Scott intercepted him with a look, and Cody reluctantly pulled his hand back.

Wondering why the boy wasn't deep-frying his brains in front of the television like other kids his age, Scott double-checked that the camera was mounted securely in the corner. From that angle, the entire room was visible. Hidden Dolby speakers on either side of the camcorder would pick up the slightest noise. He intended to leave the machine on until the following morning. All his cameras came with a night shot infrared system that could capture any image in total darkness, smoke, or fog.

He had one more camera to set up. Case in hand, he ushered Cody out of the room, shut the door, and took the stairs up to the attic at a sprint, confident the pudgy boy would be slow in following. Other than nose picking, Cody didn't seem to get much exercise.

The attic door was stuck. As in many old houses, the wood had a tendency to swell. He had to push against the door several times to open it.

The room was filled with old furniture draped in white cloth. Sunbeams slanted through the dusty window. Carefully, Scott set his camera case on the floor and pulled out a slim black machine about the size of a Palm Pilot—his EMF (electromagnetic frequency) meter.

Large fluctuations in electromagnetic fields occurred in areas where paranormal activity took place.

Sweeping the instrument in an arc around the room, he checked the readings.

A tingling began at the base of his spine.

He had already double-checked the neighborhood for power lines, underground metal deposits, and anything that could possibly account for unusual levels of electro-magnetic energy, but he'd discovered nothing out of the ordinary.

Which meant that the high fluctuation in electromag-netic frequency the meter was picking up now originated in the attic.

Excitement welled inside him. However, since Wilders were not prone to excessive enthusiasm (exhibiting such emotion was considered bad form), Scott merely allowed himself a small smile.

The door burst open and Cody stomped into the room, cheeks flushed, breathing pronounced. Out of curiosity, Scott aimed the meter at the boy, but the readings were normal. So Cody wasn't the spawn of Satan.

Scott had to check.

Cody continued to wheeze. "I've . . . heard," he gasped, "some of the . . . strange noises too."

A second witness to paranormal phenomena?

Any *spookologist* worth his salt would want to know more.

"You have? Describe the sounds for me," Scott asked.

Cody stepped up to the wall, curled his hand into a fist, and started knocking. Then he curved his fingers into the plaster and began scraping the wall. Obviously enjoying himself, Cody changed from scraping to banging. Scott winced.

Despite the boy's unnecessary roughness, he knew the re-creation was accurate. The sounds of hollow knocking and loud scratching, as if someone were trying to claw his way out from behind the wall, were classic signs of a haunting. Parapsychology 101.

Cody continued banging on the wall. "You can stop now," Scott said. Cody ignored him and added kicking to his repertoire.

Scott checked the EMF meter again, just to make sure Cody hadn't scared away a possible spirit.

The readings were still high.

The kicking and banging stopped. "Do you feel that?" Cody whispered.

The cold descended upon them.

Then came the goose bumps.

Each of the soft hairs on the back of Scott's neck quivered and stood on end.

Friends and relatives frequently teased Scott, asking if he spent all his time in dusty old attics, chasing Casper.

He looked down at the EMF meter. The machine confirmed what he already knew.

Casper was here.

3

Coulter

Bitterroot, Idaho

Coulter Marshall figured the old saying applied to the giant in front of him. The man had fallen out of the ugly tree and hit every branch on the way down.

Gritting his teeth, directing all his force to his right arm, Coulter pushed up as hard as he could. Beads of sweat broke out on his forehead. He was losing and the jackasses in the bar were cheering.

The hulking figure of the man across the table from him effortlessly applied more pressure and signaled the bartender for another shot with his free arm.

Cocky bastard.

Coulter was now in considerable pain. But he needed

the money. He needed warm weather. He needed to get the hell out of Idaho.

His arm was almost to the table. The hulk grinned and squeezed harder than he had to. Coulter clenched his jaw. The heavily tattooed, shaved-head son of a bitch—bless his heart—was trying to break the bones in his hand and having a good time doing it. Any moment now Coulter would be handicapped for life. Worse, he'd be out two hundred bucks.

Once again, he pondered the wisdom of his chosen career. Walking into dives like this and challenging the biggest, meanest wastes of skin to a feat of strength was not a well-paying gig. But Coulter didn't have any other talents, other than being able to move shit with his mind.

Time to use the well-worn, tried-and-true, Marshall Method.

First, he had to find an object on or near the ugly beast. The man's boots? Nah. What would he do, pull the laces tight? The snakeskin belt? He could try to cut off his air. And then he knew.

Coulter concentrated on the table between them. It wasn't going to be hard. He was angry. It always worked best when he was angry.

He focused and felt the familiar pull as if some invisible magnet was drawing him in. Slowly, the table began to move. The Hulk looked down in surprise. No one else noticed, and Coulter wanted to keep it that way.

It would have been a damn sight easier, Coulter often reflected, if he could actually move people with his mind, but for some reason he could only control objects and not living things.

He had ventured into the local library once and discovered his ability was known as telekinesis. He also discovered that most scientists believed telekinesis, telepathy, and other so-called powers did not exist. Why the hell then, Coulter wondered, did scientists spend all that time thinking up names like telekinesis?

Meanwhile, focusing hard while fighting to keep his arm from touching the table was not the easiest task. The table moved up slightly into the air and shifted until one of the legs settled on the Hulk's foot. He then concentrated hard—not enough to crack bone, but the crushing pain must have been intense.

The Hulk howled and loosened his grip. Coulter seized the advantage. He slammed the man's meaty arm to the table. There was a hushed silence and then a roar from the crowd. Coulter released the table leg, and the pull in his gut disappeared.

The Hulk opened his mouth. "No! He didn't win! My foot was—"

"The little guy really did it," someone said.

In his defense, Coulter thought "little" a bit extreme. At twenty-six, he stood five feet, eleven inches tall with a narrow waist, thick golden hair, blue eyes, and, according to his mother, the face of an angel that hid the devil inside.

Coulter would easily pass muster anywhere else, but in this bar in the Idaho wilderness filled with bikers, survivalists, and lumberjacks, he seemed almost feminine . . . which now explained the uncomfortable incident with the miner in the urinal.

"He cheated," the Hulk yelled. "Something happened to the table."

Coulter swiped the wad of money off the table and widened his blue eyes innocently. "Prove it," he said.

They never could.

Putting on his white Stetson, Coulter threw on his denim jacket and slipped out into the cold, dark night. He headed straight for the bus station.

4

Parapsychology Department
Mill University
Oakland, California

Mill University's parapsychology department was housed in an old ivy-covered building on the edge of campus, tucked as far away from proper academia as possible. The building was so old that Scott thought the ivy was the only thing holding it up.

Academic stepchild or not, the department had the facilities to carry out cattle-call psychic testing, inviting anyone who believed he had an overdeveloped sixth sense to come in and be evaluated. That's why Scott was there.

The Greta Evans case had been an easy one—barring the annoying, albeit useful, presence of her grandson, Cody.

Greta had been thrilled with the news that her house was haunted. "Let Mimi Perkins have her brand-new living room set. I've got a real live ghost!" she'd crowed. Future clients, however, might not take too kindly to a ghostly roommate, especially a malevolent one. And there was only one way to cleanse the house of a spirit. Make contact. For that he would need a medium.

The building had the musty smell of an old library, and Scott's steps echoed hollowly as he headed up to the second floor. His destination was the observation booth. He found Eddie there, seated and observing a test in progress. In his early fifties, short and squat, with a gruff manner and thick head of gray hair, Dr. Edward Mirza looked more like a bookie than a man who'd devoted his life to the study of the paranormal. "I've seen more psychic potential on Dionne Warwick's network," Eddie grumbled as Scott laughed and dropped down into the seat next to him.

Eddie shot him an appreciative look. "So you finally opened up your own firm? I knew that paper trading or dollar shuffling or whatever the hell you were doing in New York—"

"I was a stockbroker."

"Whatever. I knew that crap wouldn't last. This is your first love. Has been since you were a kid with a silver spoon up your butt. How'd your family take the news when you, ah, switched careers?"

Scott raised an eyebrow. "How do you think?"

Eddie grinned and cocked his head toward the glass partition. Scott leaned forward and viewed the test currently in progress. The candidate was a middle-aged woman with a thick black bun and a heavily made-up face. A casually dressed female grad student was conducting the interview.

"It's routine to ask a few background questions first," Eddie said. "Sometimes you can eliminate the crazies just from that."

A fact Scott was well aware of. He was having a devil of a time trying to find psychics to employ in his firm. He'd combed the records of the ASPR (American Society for Psychical Research), the reports of well-known parapsychologists, and he'd compiled a record of every reported paranormal event in the known world dating back fifty years.

Unfortunately, most of the people he'd interviewed had leaned more toward the psychotic rather than the psychic.

Eddie raised the volume on the intercom, and the voices inside the testing room came through loud and clear.

"Madame Zola, when did you first realize you have psychic ability?" the grad student asked.

Madame Zola? If the madame could prove she had even a drop of Gypsy blood running through her veins, Scott would quit the firm, marry a woman named Bunny, and start spending Sundays at the country club.

Madame Zola answered, "When I was five and correctly predicted the neighbor's cat, Dingleberry, would return home."

"Interesting, and how did—"

"Then the world discovered my ability the day I predicted President Clinton would be assassinated."

"Former President Clinton is very much alive."

"He most certainly is not!" Madame Zola glared through thick gobs of mascara.

"Is too . . ."

"Clinton is dead. The Republicans put a curse on his head. And I'm the one who predicted it! Not Jeane Dixon! Me!"

The grad student closed the folder on her desk and smiled tightly. "Thank you, we'll let you know."

"Amateurs!" Madame Zola sniffed and exited the room with offended dignity.

Eddie turned to Scott. "You-know-who is going to be plenty pissed when she finds you here."

"That's a chance I'll have to take. I had to ask you in person—"

Eddie drew in a sharp breath. "Too late."

Scott turned to see a tall, statuesque redhead in an Armani suit heading toward them.

Dr. Vivica Bates.

The author of a number of commercially successful books on the paranormal, Vivica was considered an authority on psychic phenomena.

Scott considered her a blood-sucking she-bat from hell.

They'd first met back when Scott was a freshman at Stanford and Vivica had been invited by the university to deliver a lecture on parapsychology. Sitting in the darkened Clark Center auditorium, Scott had been thrilled to find someone as passionate about psychic phenomena as he was. With her stunning looks and vibrant coloring, the spotlight making her translucent skin glow, Vivica held him in thrall. Afterwards he asked her out for coffee. She insisted on Scotch. Their affair began that very night.

Alas, a few weeks later Scott discovered Vivica on her office desk under the dean of social sciences. It was quite obvious the two weren't discussing the origins of psychokinesis. Scott ended the relationship on the spot. Vivica chided him for being melodramatic, and the dean struggled to zip up his pants.

Needless to say, the couple did not part on the healthiest of terms.

Vivica didn't waste any time on pleasantries. "What the hell are you doing here, Wilder?"

Scott's gaze was cool as it traveled the length of her figure. "Nice to see your hair grew back after that episode with the pyrokinetic."

Vivica narrowed her eyes. "Could this visit be because of your so-called firm?" She reached into her jacket pocket and drew out a folded newspaper clipping.

Scott recognized it as the ad he'd placed in the *Chronicle*. "What have you been doing? Carrying that thing around in the hopes you'd run into me?"

Ignoring him, she began to read. " 'The Cold Spot: Paranormal Investigations Firm.' The Cold Spot? How childishly clever."

Eddie thumped Scott on the shoulder and laughed. "I like it."

Vivica rolled her eyes. "Of course you would, Mirza. Maybe Wilder here can make you up a T-shirt and matching baseball cap with the logo."

"What's the matter, Vivica?" Scott asked. "Afraid of a little competition?"

"*Little* being the operative word." She crumpled up the clipping and flicked it with one long, manicured red nail, hitting the trash can dead center. She turned back to him, her green eyes flashing. "Oh, and if I catch you anywhere near my office or using any of the equipment, I'll alert my friends at campus security. So do your socializing somewhere else." She swept past the observation booth, into her office, and slammed the door.

"Well that went well," Scott murmured.

Eddie sighed and shook his head. "Sorry about that, pal, but she's head of the department."

A moment later three men in dark suits, white shirts, and black ties came into the room.

Eddie lowered his voice. "Vivica's minions."

The minions weren't alone. A pale sliver of a man huddled in their midst. As they passed by, the slight man turned and focused his gray eyes on Scott. It was like looking into a funhouse mirror, cold, metallic, twisted, and somehow wrong.

Scott shivered. "Who was that?"

"That, my friend, is Hans Morden—Vivica's latest discovery. His psi readings are off the charts."

Scott recalled the look in Hans's gray eyes. "The man's unstable. He and Vivica are welcome to each other."

In the observation room another candidate was being interviewed. The grad student—looking worse for wear—was administering the Rhine test using a deck of Zener cards, twenty-five cards each imprinted with one of five symbols. She held up a card with the symbol of a star. "What am I seeing?"

The subject—a man with long, greasy hair and three hoop earrings in his left ear—cocked his head and scratched his armpit. "Sammy Sosa?"

"Once again, this is not a deck of baseball cards."

"Ah . . . Babe Ruth?"

Scott ignored the clairvoyantly challenged hippie and turned to Eddie. "Remember that tidy sum I helped you make on the market? I need a favor . . ."

5

The Sunset Grill just off Union Square featured light jazz music, rose decor, an extensive wine list, and an open kitchen where patrons could watch the staff prepare their dinner—and presumably check that their entrée was not stepped in, spit on, or spiked with salmonella.

But in Anjali's opinion, the best thing about the place was the atmosphere.

It had none.

Hard to do in a city drenched in history like San Francisco, where the haunted past was alive and well. She couldn't imagine strolling through Athens, Rome, or Jerusalem, ancient cities still holding on to their ghosts, where even the buildings had moods. Tough on a telepath.

No, the Sunset Grill had no soul.

And she loved it.

Anjali took a sip of her cocktail and tried to ignore the disapproval etched into her older sister's thin face.

"You do know how fattening vodka is, don't you?" Zarina asked. "And tonic water is loaded with calories."

"It's good fat," Anjali replied and took another sip.

The dinner wasn't a social visit. Last year their father had accepted chairmanship of the math department at Tempe University, even though it meant relocating to Arizona and only a slight wage increase. Then again, their father would have relocated to Homer, Alaska, if it meant a slight wage increase.

So with their parents now living in another state, Zarina had assumed the role of parental substitute. Even though nobody had asked her to.

Her sister looked more disapproving than ever, so Anjali turned to her brother-in-law, Vijay. He was almost as thin as his wife, tended to blink excessively, and already had, at thirty-three, the hunched posture of an old man.

Vijay was currently blinking at his BlackBerry, typing rapidly with his thumbs. He had yet to touch the unsweetened decaffeinated iced tea Zarina had ordered for him.

Anjali wondered what kind of e-mails Vijay was getting that needed his immediate attention. The man was a podiatrist. Did somebody out there truly and desperately need his advice or opinion? Someone with toe deformities or an outbreak of fatal foot fungus?

"How's the job search going?" Zarina asked.

Several weeks ago, Anjali's job as a computer programmer at BayTech had been outsourced to India. The fact that her parents had immigrated to America seeking greater employment opportunities, and now, decades later, their daughter's employment opportunities were being shipped off to India, was not lost on Anjali.

She found the irony astounding.

"I haven't exactly been looking for a job," she replied.

"Why not?"

"Because in San Jose you can't throw a motherboard without hitting a programmer, and then having that programmer install an update and throw it back at you. Not to mention the competition coming from India, where programmers do your job in half the time for half the salary, and every rickshaw comes outfitted with a wireless Internet connection. Besides, computer programming isn't as fulfilling as I thought it would be."

Zarina frowned. "But what else are you going to do?"

What was she going to do?

Anjali was rounding thirty, without friends, without a significant other, and without any discernible talents. Sure, she could program, and then there was the whole ESP thing. Not that she was contemplating a career as a psychic.

She couldn't read palms, tea leaves, or coffee grounds. She couldn't tell the future, and she had doubts whether anyone really could. So what could she do? It wasn't like there was a section on ESP in *What Color Is Your Parachute?*

Not even in the new edition!

She was a medium. She had a direct line to the spirit world. But so what? This wasn't the Hollywood version. The thoughts and emotions of the dead came to her, but often they were so garbled, she couldn't make head or tail of the experience.

Anjali often wondered if human beings lost the power of clarity after death.

"I'll make some calls at work tomorrow," Zarina said. "I'm pretty sure the biomechanics lab has an opening for a programmer."

The last thing Anjali wanted was to spend five days a week under the disapproving gaze of her sister. And what was biomechanics anyway? Didn't Zarina have a Ph.D. in biochemistry?

Anjali was saved from making a lame excuse by the arrival of the waiter. He set their orders down on the table: two vegetarian portobello pizzas made with nondairy soy cheese, and one steak medium-rare with a side of fries.

Guess which dish was for her.

Anjali felt like a hypocrite ordering the steak. Not because she was Hindu, but because she belonged to an organization devoted to animal rights, and she was the only nonvegetarian member. She didn't know how to explain herself. All she knew was that she couldn't stand to see an animal being cruelly treated and she couldn't turn down a well-cut side of beef.

Call her a hypocrite, call her complex, and she'd call you when she finally figured herself out.

Vijay slammed his BlackBerry on the table, causing nearby heads to turn. "I've changed my e-mail half a dozen times but I keep getting spammed. Ads for low-interest home mortgages, triple-strength Viagra, how to increase your sperm count—"

Anjali laughed.

"—and psychic advice."

The laughter died in her throat. Across the table, Zarina froze.

Still absorbed with his spam issues, Vijay didn't notice

the emotional byplay. But then why should he? Vijay didn't know Anjali was psychic. Zarina had sworn her to secrecy.

Now looking at her sister's rigid face, Anjali felt her cheeks grow warm. She knew the root of her family's behavior stemmed from fear. Fear of the unknown. Fear of what people would say when they discovered her peculiarity. She had some of those same fears herself.

Didn't stop her from being annoyed with her family, though.

Zarina placed her napkin on the table and excused herself. Anjali sat back and stared glumly at the table.

"Ah . . ." Vijay leaned forward and peered with interest at her plate. "Can I have a French fry?"

A little startled, Anjali nevertheless pushed her plate toward him. "Dig in."

Vijay looked over his shoulder, realized the coast was clear, then stuffed a bunch of fries into his mouth. He closed his eyes and chewed. "Now that's good. Not as good as the fries at Frjtz though." He blinked at her. "I can let you in on a little insider tip. Burger King has the best fries—if you go between one and one-thirty. That's when they change the grease traps. McDonald's used to be good until they were sued by a bunch of Brahmins and forced to remove the beef tallow."

So Vijay had a closet fry addiction—the more beef tallow, the better. Anjali smiled, feeling a sense of camaraderie with her brother-in-law. She decided to take a risk and leaned forward, resting her elbows on the table—Emily Post be damned—and kept her voice casual. "What *do* you think of psychic advice and all that Shirley MacLaine stuff?" Fry halfway to his mouth, Vijay paused and looked at her. "You know, just out of curiosity," she added.

Vijay popped the fry into his mouth and chewed, a thoughtful expression on his face. "Science hasn't conclusively disproved the existence of psychic phenomena. For all we know there may be genuine psychics out there. Who's to say? Any ketchup?"

Anjali pushed the bottle toward him, then stood and mumbled something about the restroom. Busy with condiments, Vijay barely looked up.

She moved with quick steps toward the ladies' room and found her sister at the head of a line of women, preparing to step into the vacated bathroom.

Zarina's eyes widened as Anjali pushed her way inside—amid a chorus of angry protests—and locked the door behind them. "What are you doing?"

Instead of answering, Anjali stood dumbstruck as she took in the pink linoleum, the pink tile counter, and the pink poodle wallpaper. She shook her head and refocused. "Vijay is more open-minded than you think. He believes psychic abilities might exist!"

Zarina gasped, "You didn't tell him—"

"No. But that's my point! You don't have to worry. We can tell Vijay the truth. He might even think it's cool!" She knew she was probably getting excited over nothing, but it was like a knot inside her had finally loosened. If Vijay accepted her, then Zarina was bound to. Maybe they'd start acting like real sisters—confiding in each other, gossiping together, going shopping—not that they could ever borrow each other's clothes. Zarina wore a size zero, and Anjali . . . well never mind.

"No!" Zarina shouted. "You can't tell him anything!"

Anjali had never heard her sister raise her voice before and took a step back.

Zarina stood there, clenching her fists, her face white.

Anjali raised her hands and tried for a soothing voice. "I'm not going to walk up to Vijay and offer to contact his dead relatives. I'm just saying you don't have to worry so much about his reaction if I did. You don't have to worry that your husband will condemn you because of me."

Zarina sighed, some of the tension leaving her body. "You don't understand. It's more complicated than that."

Anjali made sure the pink toilet lid was down before taking a seat. "Understand what?"

"Remember Uncle Gopal? He used to preach Hindu-Muslim brotherhood. He wanted India and Pakistan to be friends."

Anjali nodded. "He used to say Allah and Krishna were one. He even wrote a song about it and performed it at parties." She remembered her uncle sporting a jaunty red beret and breaking out the accordion before each performance.

Zarina leaned back against the sink. "And then one day our cousin, Priya, comes home with her new boyfriend—Tariq. An exchange student from Karachi."

"He threw both of them out of the house and told Priya he'd disown her. But that doesn't mean—"

"Yes it does." Now Zarina was trying for the soothing voice. "People can be very liberal about things until it hits close to home. Like that movie *Guess Who's Coming to Dinner*. But minus the happy ending."

Anjali guessed she'd been cast in the Sidney Poitier role. The knot inside her was back and tighter than ever.

Meanwhile, Zarina still had to use the bathroom and did not want an audience.

6

$\int$omewhere along the Idaho and Nevada border, Coulter found himself on a deserted stretch of road in the middle of a small, dusty town.

"What a shit hole," he muttered, lighting a cigarette.

The bus ticket out of Idaho had gotten him this far. Now he just had to decide whether to head south to Vegas or west to San Francisco and farther on to L.A. He didn't have a particular destination in mind. He never did. Not since that sunny Tennessee day his mother claimed raising a son was cramping her lifestyle and kicked him out of the double wide. He'd been fifteen.

With no family to speak of and not wanting to end up in foster care, Coulter took off. In the beginning, he worked odd jobs, barely living off what he earned, but then one day the carnival came to Chattanooga. He decided to try his luck at knocking down three milk bottles stacked in a triangle. His first three shots just glanced off the bottles and failed to knock down a single one. Annoyed, he purchased three more balls and failed twice more.

By this time Coulter figured out that even a hurricane blowing through the lot wouldn't knock over a damn bottle. Thoroughly ticked at getting conned, his anger grew. He felt the pull in his gut and hurled his last ball at the target. Not only did the ball knock down the milk bottles but the shelf of prizes behind it as well, and tore a hole in the tent. Coulter walked off with a good chunk of the carny's money, and a whole new career was born.

God smiled down on Coulter Marshall that day.

He hadn't heard from the Man since.

Eleven years later, he was still drifting.

Only now he was looking for bigger game, higher stakes. The kind of score he could coast on for months instead of days. He needed a big city for that. But first he needed a drink.

And like every other crap-hole town in blessed America that didn't possess a hospital, library, or ethnic diversity, this one had a bar.

He stubbed out his cigarette, pushed open the door, and let his eyes adjust to the darkness. When he noticed the three men playing pool in the corner, his lips curved in a smile and his gaze took on a predatory gleam.

He'd have his drink and make a few bucks in the process.

Coulter walked up to the bar and sat down. He took off his Stetson, laid it on the counter, and ran his fingers through his blond hair.

The bartender was a woman in her early forties, he

guessed. Who the hell knew a woman's age these days anyway? You had sixty-year-old women Botoxed to look thirty and sixteen-year-olds dolled up to look twenty-five.

The woman tossed her unnaturally bright red hair and surveyed him with a hand on her hip. "Hey there, cowboy, haven't seen anyone as handsome as you walk through that door before."

"Today's your lucky day, Red."

"Name's Loretta. What'll you have?"

"Whiskey. Straight up."

She set the glass before him. "We don't get too many strangers here. Where you from?"

Coulter took a swallow of his drink before answering. He'd spun so many lies upon lies that even the simplest question took careful thought. He decided that in this case the truth couldn't hurt. "Tennessee."

"What are you doing here?"

"Passing through."

Loretta smiled and took the hint, turning away to polish a row of shot glasses. Coulter focused his attention back to the pool players.

He could hardly tell them apart, what with their scruffy beards, greasy hair, and bad teeth.

Coulter caught Loretta's eye and angled his head toward the men. "What's up with the cast from *Deliverance*? Locals?"

She nodded. "They work over at the gypsum mine. Act like a bunch of drunken sailors. Come in every Friday and blow their paycheck. Naturally"—she grinned—"I'm not complaining."

Today was Friday.

Well bless their hearts, Coulter thought. Piss drunk with a paycheck. Just the way he liked 'em.

Downing his whiskey, he headed over to the pool table. "How about a game?"

One of the men smirked. "You don't look strong enough to lift a cue stick, pretty boy." The other two snickered and elbowed each other.

"I can do more than lift it, Cletus. Care to wager?"

Cletus scowled. "You any good?"

"Yeah," Coulter lied.

"You tryin' to hustle us?"

Coulter shrugged. "Well now, that all depends on whether I win or not."

The three men looked at one another and then back at him.

"If you'd rather not venture," Coulter said, "seein' as how you'd probably lose your money to me anyway." He turned to leave.

"Let Goldilocks play a game," one of the men said.

Coulter turned back and took off his denim jacket, tossing it onto a bar stool. He held out his hand for a cue stick. "Rack 'em and crack 'em, boys."

Unlike most pool sharks, Coulter had the unique distinction of being truly terrible at the game.

That was the idea.

Playing honestly and as skillfully as he could, he lost the first two games.

In between roaring with laughter and calling Coulter names, the men continued to pound beers.

Coulter ordered another whiskey and placed his remaining money on the table. "One more match," he said. "Double or nothin'."

Loretta walked over with his drink. "You sure, hon?"

He tipped the contents into his mouth and handed her the empty glass. "It'll be just fine."

Once again the table was racked. This time Coulter broke.

Concentrating, he felt the familiar pull in his gut and guided the seven and five balls straight into the pocket.

No need to overdo it. Telekinesis required a fine touch.

Unconcerned, Cletus took his shot, eyes widening as the ball veered slightly off course.

Coulter almost laughed.

For the remainder of the game, each of Cletus's shots just barely missed the pocket. In one case, the ball stopped right before the pocket and rolled back.

So Coulter didn't always exercise a fine touch; sometimes he just had fun.

The third game went to him.

Cletus demanded a rematch. "Hell if that wasn't just dumb luck on your side. Double or nothin'."

Coulter chalked his cue stick. "Always happy to oblige."

He won the next game as well.

Cletus kicked the wall. "Goddamn it!"

Wallet sufficiently padded, Coulter decided to hit the road. "Nice playin' with you, boys," he called out and grabbed his Stetson. Arms folded across her chest, Loretta smiled at him. He pulled out a fifty-dollar bill and slapped it on the bar. "Thanks for the drinks, Red."

Her smile widened. "Any time, gorgeous."

Grinning, Coulter turned around and stopped as Cletus and his two hayseeds maneuvered themselves in front of the door. "You're not thinkin' of leavin', are you, pretty boy?"

"You call me pretty boy one more time and I'll start thinkin' you've got a thing for me," Coulter said.

Cletus glared. "Give us our money."

Coulter didn't bat a blue eye. "We had an *honest* wager, boys. Wouldn't be gentlemanly of ya'll to forget that."

He'd dealt with this kind of thing before. People didn't take kindly to parting with their money by honest or dishonest means. He scanned the room, looking for something he could *use*. Something with weight. The heavy fluorescent light fixture above the door caught his eye. He focused, and it began to sway.

Just then he heard an all-too-familiar sound. The bolt being pulled back on a shotgun. He stiffened.

Loretta stood behind the bar, shotgun raised in her hands. "The man won his money fair and square, boys. Now let him on his way."

"Come on, Loretta, that's our money for the rest of the week," Cletus whined.

Loretta's hands were steady on the rifle. "Then I bet you feel real stupid now, don't ya?" she said.

Grumbling, all three men stepped away from the door.

Coulter was sure the surprise showed on his face. No one had ever defended him before. There was a sour taste in his mouth. He didn't like it.

Tasted like guilt.

Loretta cocked her head toward the door. "Go on now. I hope it was worth it."

With a final wave, Coulter walked out into the evening sky. Staring up at the orange and purple clouds, he thought about the money in his pocket.

Was it worth it?

For the first time, he didn't think it was.

7

Anjali knew she was being followed.

She wouldn't be much of a telepath if she didn't.

He'd followed her from the pet food section and kept his distance as she maneuvered her cart between rows of liquor.

Anjali was out of staples like cat food and vodka.

Ah, the life of a single psychic gal in the city.

She was tempted to lead her pursuer on a wild-goose chase—ducking in and out of buildings, zigzagging across streets, leaping on and off buses—but she was feeling lazy.

Besides, she wasn't getting any serial killer vibes from him.

She lifted a blue bottle of Skyy off the shelf and turned around to put it in her cart and came face to face with her supermarket stalker.

His smile was hesitant. "Anjali?"

He had nice teeth—white and straight. Anjali had a thing about teeth. You could be the most attractive person in the world, but if your teeth were funky—forget about it.

He also pronounced her name correctly. Most people tended to say An-jelly, when it was really Un-ja-lee.

Nevertheless, she didn't make a habit of fraternizing with strange men just because they practiced good dental hygiene and happened to pronounce her name correctly.

"Yes?" she said with just a touch of surly.

Anjali did not subscribe to the notion that a stranger was a friend you hadn't met yet.

"My name is Scott Wilder. Sorry about approaching you like this but your phone has call blocker and, well . . . never mind." He held out his business card. "This should explain why I'm here."

She didn't want to take it, but figured the faster she got this over with, the faster he'd leave. So she put down the bottle and took the card.

The Cold Spot
Paranormal Investigations
Scott Wilder: Founder

The Cold Spot? She had to admit that was pretty clever. Still, she didn't make a habit of fraternizing with paranormal investigators just because they were good with words.

"I'm sorry," she said, handing back his card. "But I'm not interested."

"Let me explain—"

She tried to keep her voice even. "Listen, being psychic

isn't a gift. It's a curse. I've spent my whole life avoiding anything to do with the supernatural, the paranormal, whatever you want to call it. So you're just wasting your time."

He held her gaze for a few moments and then smiled again. "You know, I need a few groceries myself." He took hold of her cart. "Mind if I share yours? Call it cart pooling. Less traffic in the aisle." He headed off toward the produce department.

Anjali frowned. Persistent, he was.

Scott Wilder was thumping a cantaloupe when she approached. "That's a keeper. Did you know the Australian aborigines think of telepathy as a normal human function?"

"If an aborigine jumped off a cliff, would you?" Determined, she took hold of the cart and moved away. Scott followed her, cantaloupe tucked under his arm.

"Aren't you curious about how I found you?" he asked.

"No." She pushed her cart past the beauty care aisle and saw a woman trying to shove two boxes of hair dye under her shirt.

"Personally, I prefer a bigger shirt when I go shoplifting," Scott murmured. "That way I can get in at least a week's worth of groceries."

Anjali almost laughed as she pushed the cart forward. She was trying to thaw out from the frozen food section when she noticed Scott was nowhere to be seen. Good riddance, she thought, and finished the rest of her shopping.

Standing in line to pay, Anjali was hopelessly eavesdropping on the squabbling couple in front of her, when Scott showed up lugging a full basket. Her surprise must have shown on her face because he grinned.

"I really did need a few things."

Anjali found some of her annoyance toward him dissipating. She turned a curious eye to his basket. Alfalfa sprouts, celery hearts, whole grain bread, and of course the cantaloupe. A health nut. Her sister, Zarina, would love him. Well, except for the whole "investigating the supernatural" thing.

"I know you don't really care," Scott said. "But it was Mill University."

So that was how he'd found her. Anjali shook her head in disgust. "Jesus, you take one ESP test and you're on their list forever."

"The file mentioned the Bradford House and the . . . incident. You were on a class field trip?"

"Social studies. The house wasn't supposed to be haunted—not like the Winchester. It wasn't even that historic. The descendants had made a bunch of changes—installing indoor plumbing and fixing a broken sewage line—and that upset the local historical society."

The corner of Scott's mouth quirked up in a smile. "Naturally. The preservation of history supersedes sanitation."

"That's always been my motto," Anjali said and then looked at him, narrowing her eyes. "You do realize that just because I'm talking to you, doesn't mean I want anything to do with you."

Scott put the basket down and flexed his hands. "Of course. I just assumed you'd already scanned the headlines of the *Star* and the *Globe* and had nothing else to do."

"Now that we understand each other . . ." Anjali pushed her groceries together, making room for Scott to lay his on the checkout counter. "Anyway," she continued, keeping a close eye that his sprouts didn't touch her Cheetos, "I didn't have a sense, not even a clue that anything was wrong until I walked into the house. Then it was like being . . . invaded. Emotions and thoughts that weren't mine filled me up. I felt overshadowed. I could smell death."

"What does death smell like?" Scott asked.

She shrugged. "Atlantic City."

His dark eyes flashed with amusement.

Anjali looked away. She could joke about it now. Had to joke about it. If it wasn't for her sense of humor, she would have killed herself . . . twice.

"I must have blacked out," she continued. "When I woke up I was in the hospital and somebody from the university was there to talk to me."

"According to the file, the attending doctor in the ER arranged that."

"My parents were furious when they found out. My mother cursed the doctor out in Hindi. Although I'm still not sure why calling someone 'a dirty owl' is bad."

Anjali often thanked God that she wasn't an only child. If all her parents' hopes and dreams had depended on her they would have committed suicide . . . twice.

"I'd really like your input on this case," Scott said in a cautious voice. "You're older now and—"

"Don't you get it? I'm afraid of ghosts! Nothing you can say or do will ever convince me otherwise. Why don't you call John Edward? He loves talking to the dead. Apparently he's got them on speed dial."

Scott's upper lip curled. "John Edward? Don't get me started."

At the scent of scandal, Anjali's ears perked. "What? Have you met him?"

"I'll tell you another time," Scott said. "Oh right . . . we won't be working together."

The register next to them opened up. Scott grabbed his basket and neatly maneuvered to the head of the line.

Meanwhile, Anjali's line continued to move like a clogged artery, and the couple in front of her continued to argue.

"God, you're cheap," the woman snapped.

The man glared. "I'm nothing but a prick and a pay-check. Is that it?"

Anjali watched as Scott grabbed his bags and sailed out the exit.

She hated ghost hunters.

Even if they did call themselves paranormal investigators.

$\mathcal{C}$oulter was at a diner called Lenny's off Mission Street in San Francisco.

The lighting was fluorescent, the booths plastic, and the servers unmotivated.

But it was nearly two A.M., and the sign outside claimed the place served a steak and eggs breakfast all day. He was starving.

He'd spent most of the day wandering around the city and nearly freezing his ass off even though it was July. He'd avoided all the touristy places after being mowed down by a baby carriage . . . several baby carriages, in fact, wielded by parents who had the same crazy look in their eyes soldiers probably had as they drove a tank straight through enemy lines.

The enemy in this case being people who were fortunate

enough not to have a brat swinging from their arm or drooling down their neck.

And sometimes—although he didn't like to admit it—being in those places, alongside families in lame matching T-shirts eating anything fried on a stick, made him feel lonely.

He gazed around at the other people in the restaurant. There were only a few. In one of the booths a cadaverous-looking woman with long white hair and bloodred lipstick sat next to an overweight man wearing an eye patch and a black velvet skirt.

"Freaks," he murmured.

Then again, he got his kicks spinning silverware around in the air when inclined, so maybe he shouldn't go around labeling people.

He looked back at the couple and shook his head. Nah, anyway you looked at it, they were freaks.

Earlene, the blue-haired octogenarian who'd seated him, brought over his food. Before she could leave, he touched her arm and smiled. "Can I get a side of hash browns, love?"

Earlene beamed and patted his cheek. "Coming right up."

Digging into his meal, he wolfed down his food and was almost halfway through when a shout made him look up.

At the counter, a short, stocky man with black hair, dressed in flashy but unflattering clothes, roughly pushed away his coffee cup, making it rattle in its plate. He glared at the pretty but nervous waitress. "I wanted my coffee black. There's about an udder full of milk in here."

"But you asked for—"

"I'm lactose intolerant. That means I can't digest dairy, sweetheart."

The waitress grabbed a clean cup and began filling it with coffee. "I'm sorry. I thought you asked for coffee with milk."

"I asked for coffee and the bill. Do I look like the kind of man who'd mess around with his small intestine?" He cracked open his newspaper. "I'm not paying for this coffee. My gastroenterologist is already milking me for a fortune."

Earlene returned with Coulter's plate of hash browns. "On the house, darlin'."

He took her hand and planted a kiss on the back. "Bless your heart."

She chuckled and wagged her finger at him. "You're full of charm, aren't you—you blue-eyed devil." Her voice dropped to a whisper. "Not like the character over there."

She jerked her head toward the man at the counter.

"Does Cousin Vinnie come in regularly?" Coulter asked.

She nodded. "When he isn't complaining about the food, he's trying to cozy up to Rachel."

Coulter assumed Rachel was the pretty waitress who'd served the coffee with milk.

Applying himself to his hash browns, he glanced back at the counter and caught Rachel watching him. She smiled shyly and turned away.

A slow smile spread across his face.

Well now.

Maybe his time in San Francisco wouldn't be wasted after all.

He decided to hang around until the place closed. Maybe he'd walk Rachel home. That would be the gentlemanly thing to do.

Since he was sticking around, he ordered a slice of apple pie.

From the corner of his eye he noticed Rachel watching him again. She tucked a lock of hair behind her ear, smoothed the skirt of her uniform, and edged around the counter, obviously coming toward him.

As she passed by Cousin Vinnie, he reached out and grabbed her arm, murmuring something in her ear. Her cheeks bloomed red and Rachel yanked her arm away. Then she turned and fled into the ladies' room.

Coulter didn't hesitate. Praying the coffee was still hot, he focused on the man's cup. It teetered on the edge of the saucer before abruptly shooting across the counter and into the man's lap.

With a howl he leaped off the stool, grabbing his crotch. "Christ!" He glared at Earlene, who stood watching the spectacle with obvious glee. "Don't just stand there. Move your fat ass and get me a towel."

Coulter focused again, and the buttons popped off the man's blue polyester pants, causing them to slide down his hairy legs and pool around his ankles.

Several of the waitresses and customers broke into laughter.

Sputtering with fury, he yanked up his pants and pushed his way out of the restaurant.

Smiling, Coulter sat back and finished the rest of his pie.

9

The sun was shining. The birds were chirping. And Anjali smelled like Clorox.

She was scrubbing the kitchen sink, and the bleach fumes were making her giddy. So it took her a moment or two to realize someone was knocking on the door.

She wasn't expecting anyone, but old Mrs. Griego, who lived on the fifth floor, tended to buzz anyone and everyone into the building. Last week she'd buzzed in a member from the Church of Hemp and Hallelujah.

But her visitor wasn't a churchgoer with a goofy grin. It was Scott Wilder.

Anjali knew this without opening the door.

No, it wasn't the psychic thing. She looked through the spy hole.

Hands on her hips, she pondered her next move.

"Anjali," he called out, his voice muffled by the door. "I know you're in there. Can we talk?"

I'd rather sniff Clorox, she thought.

"I'll just keep coming back," he said finally.

She opened the door. "Do I need to turn you down in Hindi? You obviously don't understand English."

Scott was wearing the same smile from the day before. "You can say it to me in any language. I don't take no for an answer. They taught us that in business school."

Anjali didn't want to carry on a conversation in the hall. Mrs. Griego probably had her big ear pressed flat against the floorboards. So she stepped aside and waved him in.

She did this with a big show of reluctance.

Still smiling, Scott walked in, a slim leather folder tucked under his arm. She hadn't noticed his clothes yesterday, but today he was dressed in a light blue Oxford shirt with the sleeves rolled up and gray wool slacks so fine the material looked like silk.

Anjali was wearing tan Capri pants that made her look shorter than she was and a V-neck tee that had seen better days.

She leaned back against the door and folded her arms. "Welcome to Casa Kumar. I'd ask you to sit but I know you won't have time for that."

"What do you want to do with the rest of your life?" Scott asked.

She was caught off guard by the question. "What? I don't know." But what really unnerved her was how she'd been asking herself the same thing for days now.

Scott sighed. "Do you know how many people I've interviewed in my search to find someone with even an iota of second sight? And here you are, the real thing, and you're just hiding away, hiding all that talent. You're like a sundial in the shade."

The quip on the tip of her tongue melted away. She was at a loss for words.

Which hardly ever happened.

He extracted a disc from the leather folder. "I have something I want you to look at. Where's your DVD player?"

Sufficiently curious, she gestured toward the entertainment center. If there was one area she splurged on it was movies—Hollywood, Bollywood, and basically everything coming out of Asia. She did a lot of entertaining at home. The guest list was pretty exclusive too.

Just Anjali and her cat.

Scott crouched before the TV set and slipped the DVD in. "I taped this four days ago." Grabbing the remote, he sat back on the sofa.

Her black cat, Kali, wandered into the room and jumped up next to Scott. He reached out to pet her, stopping when she bared her teeth and hissed.

Anjali shot Kali an approving look and curled up in the recliner, tucking her legs under her. "Let me guess. Footage of a bunch of guys crawling through a haunted house wearing night vision goggles?"

Instead of replying, Scott raised the volume.

The camera panned in on a shabby family room. A woman and two children, a boy and a girl, were seated on a worn and sagging couch. "That's Lynne Michaels," Scott said. "And two of her three kids."

Face drawn, dishwater blond hair pulled back in a tight bun, Lynne cleared her throat. "We've had all the downstairs windows looked at. Everything is fixed tight, but the carpet keeps getting wet. It hasn't rained in over a month. I've had the pipes checked and there isn't a single leak."

Anjali knew where this was going. "Scott—"

"Wait, just watch a little more, please."

It was the *please* that did it. It wasn't like he was begging. But it was close.

"Fine." She leaned forward and propped her chin on her hands.

Now the little girl was speaking. "And there's noises in the walls . . . like scratching. The lights in my room won't stay on. It's always cold inside. I sleep with Mommy." She nudged her brother. "Tell them." The little boy looked down at his hands and stayed silent. "He sleeps with us too," she added.

"We've had electricians come in," Lynne said in a tired voice. "They can't find anything. The baby is at my mother's. She can't take in all of us though."

Anjali looked at Scott in dismay. "There's a baby involved? Don't tell me there's a baby involved."

Scott hit the pause button. "The strange occurrences began with the baby monitor. Strange clicks and then whispers began coming through. At first Lynne thought the monitor was picking up noises from the TV or the radio, but the kids would be in bed, nobody was downstairs. She's had items go missing, dish towels, scissors, pliers, toys."

"Why don't they move?"

"She's a single mom. It took her almost a year to find a house they could afford in a decent area. But she finally put the house up for sale weeks ago. Not a single bid. I'm telling you, anyone who walks into that house feels something's off."

Anjali didn't consider herself a dumb person, but she'd honestly never expected normal people to be affected negatively by ghosts and such. Just her. Not a single mom with three kids.

Still, Anjali didn't understand how she could possibly help. "What do you want me to do? You already suspect the house is haunted. It's not like you need me to sense anything."

Scott leaned forward, his dark gaze serious. "I want you to help me find out what's in that house and why it's there. And then I want you to tell it to leave."

10

C oulter hadn't hustled any pool, cheated anyone at cards, or challenged anyone to a rigged feat of strength.

His purpose in coming to the city—bigger cons, bigger stakes—had disappeared in the face of a pretty waitress named Rachel.

Now if only she would quit asking him what he was thinking about.

They were in her bedroom, where they'd spent the better part of the day.

Naked and nestled against his back, Rachel stretched and sighed. "What are you thinking about?" she murmured.

Coulter clenched his jaw in annoyance. "Nothing."

"You always say that."

"Because it's true. I rarely have a thought in my head. I'm not complicated, sweetheart."

Rachel pulled teasingly at one of his locks. "How come a guy gets to naturally have hair this color?"

Enough with the questions, he thought. Then decided to ask one of his own. "Why do you sleep on the floor?"

Rachel laughed. "Japanese minimalism, just a few tatami mats, some shoji screens, and the futon we're using. Leaves me clear and uncluttered and able to focus on other things." Her hand slid across his stomach and then dipped lower. "Like you for instance."

Coulter sucked in his breath. Catching her hand, he moved it away to a less sensitive area. "Give me some time to build up my strength, Lady Viagra."

Rachel was quiet after that, and Coulter relaxed. He closed his eyes.

"Do you want to see the new Brad Pitt movie?" Rachel asked.

"No," he said shortly.

"He's my favorite actor."

Coulter stubbornly kept his eyes shut.

Rachel tapped him on the shoulder. "Don't you like Brad Pitt?"

He had a feeling she was going to keep bugging him until he answered. "He's got stringy hair."

"George Clooney. Now there's—"

"What's up with that squint? Hello Popeye."

Rachel giggled. "You bitch! Russell Crowe?"

"Thick legs and a stocky frame."

"Umm, what about—"

She squealed as Coulter rolled over and pulled her on top of him.

It was obvious he wasn't going to get any sleep, and hell if he wanted to answer any more questions.

He slid his hand into her hair, curving his palm against the back of her neck as he guided her head down and took her lips with his.

A door slammed in the distance, and Rachel froze.

Coulter looked up at her. "Your roommate?"

She moved off him and pulled the covers to her chin. "She's in Tahoe."

Coulter sat up. He could practically feel the tension radiating off her body. He was about to get up and investigate when the bedroom door crashed open. A petite brunette stood there and glared at them.

He let out a deep breath and lounged back on his elbows.

The stranger looked like an elf and seemed about as harmless.

Next to him, Rachel grasped the bedsheet so tightly, her knuckles were white. "You're not supposed to be here, Liz. We're through."

Oh, so it was like that now, was it? Coulter was intrigued.

He settled in for the show. He relished the idea of a catfight. Hair pulling, scratching, and Rachel was naked. Maybe the elf would end up that way too.

Instead, she pulled out a small gun and aimed it between his legs.

Jesus Christ Almighty! The gun was killing the mood.

"What the fuck is going on here?" he demanded, sitting up.

Liz's eyes glittered. "How could you, Rachel?"

Coulter decided she no longer looked cute. She looked like a deranged pixie.

And then she pulled the trigger.

Rachel screamed. Futon filling went flying. He looked down at the hole in the sheet. The bitch nearly had him singing soprano.

"Liz, stop!" Rachel cried.

Anger welled inside him. He looked wildly around for something to use, something he could move. Nothing but those goddamn mats, some paper-thin screens, and a futon.

Frustration and fear melded with the rage inside him as Liz took aim again. Coulter was unprepared for what happened next.

Without any conscious effort, he felt the familiar pull in his gut.

Liz flew back against the wall. Her gun clattered to the floor.

Coulter stared in shock. What the hell had happened? He couldn't move people. He couldn't move animals. He'd tried. Something to do with energy fields.

Too late, he realized he could have just moved the gun from her hand.

Rachel stared at him, trembling. "What just happened?"

He leaped up and grabbed his clothes. He wasn't about to hang around for the aftermath.

And not for the first time in his life, Coulter Marshall found himself running out of a woman's house buck naked.

11

Vivica Bates was in a foul mood.

Her espresso machine was on the fritz and she'd been forced to visit one of the seven Starbucks that had cropped up in town like a virulent strain of mushroom.

She sat back in her chair and propped her long legs on the desk. She'd opened the *San Francisco Chronicle* earlier to find a scathing review of her latest book, *Phenomenal Phenomena*. She wasn't comforted by the fact that the book was a commercial success or that she had a cult following on the Internet. She wanted critical acclaim.

She wanted some goddamn respect.

At the last board of trustees meeting, several tenured members approached the chancellor and expressed concern over the continued presence of a parapsychology department on campus, the consensus being that it was detrimental to the university's academic reputation.

Vivica met with the chancellor privately and displayed a decade's worth of paranormal research (along with a generous amount of cleavage).

But the old fart remained unmoved.

The world of academia didn't care about cold spots and power surges and furniture being moved around a room by unseeing hands. They wanted definitive proof regarding paranormal existence.

All the more reason, Vivica argued, for the university to continue funding her research.

Her arguments went unheeded. The board planned to reconvene in four months, and a decision would be made then.

Vivica supposed she could branch out on her own. But she craved the prestige of a university behind her. Without it she'd be just another ghost hunter.

She had a Ph.D., damn it!

There was a soft knock at the door. Her mouth tightened. She didn't appreciate being interrupted while she was contemplating her stunning achievements, past and future. "Enter," she said coolly.

Her three assistants came in: Gaspar, Maddox, and Fitch. Vivica had a hard time telling them apart. The trio all carried Starbucks containers.

Why was she not surprised?

"Where's Hans?" she asked.

Gaspar (she assumed it was Gaspar) looked behind him. "He was right here."

Maddox (the smart one, in her opinion) left her office and returned a moment later, leading Hans by the elbow. "Someone threw a half-eaten donut in the trash. He stuffed it in his mouth before I could stop him."

Vivica rolled her eyes. Considering Hans had been living off scraps when she found him, the discarded donut must have seemed like foie gras.

She stood up and gestured for him to take a seat. Hans stared back at her.

"Oh for the love of . . ." she snapped and prodded him into the chair. The man might have been gifted but he could barely function.

Vivica leaned against her desk and folded her arms. "There's been a change in plans, boys. I intend to introduce Hans to the trustee board. That gives us four months to test and hone his abilities for my presentation. After they see him in action, they'll be throwing money at me."

"Not if they see him eating out of a trash can," Fitch said.

Vivica narrowed her eyes. "Then it's your job to play Professor Higgins. I want Hans as socially acceptable as possible. Is that clear?"

"Yes ma'am," Fitch said in a subdued voice.

Vivica smiled. "Well then, let's get started."

12

A carved wooden entrance sign informed Anjali she was in the right place.

THE COLD SPOT
PARANORMAL INVESTIGATIONS

She didn't know what she expected a ghost-hunting agency to look like, but this wasn't it.

The beautifully restored Victorian came complete with gingerbread trim, thick columns, and real turrets.

Then again, as a ghost hunter, wouldn't you want to live in a place that just oozed atmosphere? Being situated in a strip mall, between a nail spa and a Subway sandwich shop, just wouldn't be the same.

It was now just half past five, and the fog had already started to roll in from the bay.

The whole place had gothic charm going for it.

Scott was going to give her a crash course in paranormal investigating and then they'd head over to the Michaels home. Lynne didn't get off work until eighty-thirty. By then it would be dark.

Of course, Anjali thought. Can't enter a haunted house until after dark.

When she was scared she felt it in her stomach. No sweaty palms or dry mouth, just her stomach—tight and twisted.

She tried to tell herself that maybe there was nothing haunted about the place. Maybe everything had a rational explanation, and Scott was just a lazy ghost hunter who hadn't looked into everything.

But in the back of her mind she knew that wasn't true. She had the feeling Scott was thorough to the point of anal retentiveness. Somehow he'd gotten her from a firm no to a "just once."

Jeez, Anjali had never thought of herself as easy before.

She stepped up to the entrance, but before she had a chance to knock, Scott opened the door, looking incredibly cheerful.

Anjali felt nauseated.

"You made it," he said.

"Looks like."

"Let me show you around. Architecture is one of my hobbies."

Stepping into the dark, elegant interior, she looked

around in awe. The inside was gorgeous. Hardwood floors, stained glass windows, and silk draperies galore.

Upon entering, she saw a parlor immediately to the right. She followed Scott into the room, and a sigh of pleasure slipped from her lips. What an exquisite room. Rose walls matched the rose accents in the blue Bokhara carpet.

"I wanted a room for interviewing clients," he explained.

Diagonally across from the parlor was the library. The room was lined with bookshelves, and a rolling ladder was needed to reach the highest shelves. A jeweled Tiffany lamp perched on the edge of an elegant carved desk, and the fireplace had one of those ornate Victorian screens in front of it. She wandered over and looked at a few of the titles. There were books of quotations, particularly by Mark Twain and Oscar Wilde.

"Nothing reduces the fear of a haunted house more than a well-placed quip," Anjali said.

Scott laughed, gently took hold of her elbow, and resumed the rest of the tour.

Back in the hall, she stopped at the staircase leading up to the second floor and Scott's residence. She was curious about that level, but he steered her toward the left side of the house.

A hallway split the left side in two. On one side was a state-of-the-art office humming with a fax machine, several computers, a scanner, and something called a white noise generator.

On the other side was a cozy den with a mounted flat-panel TV, a comfortable sofa, cushy recliners, and an elegant teak bar stocked with her favorite vodka.

The hallway ended in a large and pleasant kitchen with a breakfast nook.

Either ghost hunting was a profitable business or Scott Wilder had another source of income.

Anjali's super psychic sense said it was the latter.

"I want to show you something," Scott said as they returned to the library.

They sat down on either side of the desk, and Scott placed a sleek black leather case between them.

"What is that? A ghost hunter's kit?" she joked.

"Exactly," Scott said. "You know what a psychic's greatest gift really is?"

"The gullible public?"

"No." He frowned. "Thoroughness. I want to be as professional about this as possible. We're going to marry psychic ability with science."

The bag loomed in front of her. Anjali wondered what would come out of it—garlic cloves, Ouija board, a pentagram, holy water, a copy of *Ghostbusters* . . . ? She stifled a giggle.

Scott unzipped the bag and pulled out a tape measure. "For checking the thickness of walls. You never know when you'll find a hidden chamber—"

"Filled with skeletal remains," she supplied.

"Possibly." He then pulled out the smallest digital camera she'd ever seen. "For indoor and outdoor photography. I want to document everything we do. Plus, this also functions as a video recorder."

He then reached in and pulled out a cell phone. "I'm sure you already have one of these but don't waste your minutes. Use this one for maintaining contact at the location."

Anjali shivered. "Are you saying we'd separate? You're never supposed to separate; haven't you watched any horror movies? For God's sake, didn't you ever watch *Scooby Doo*?"

"You remind me of Daphne."

"Tell me about the house," she said.

"Typical tract housing. Built in the 1970s. The last family lived there until recently. The wife is a retired schoolteacher and moved to San Diego to be near the daughter. The husband passed away in the house. Suffered a silent heart attack at eighty-one. Died in his sleep. Happy marriage, happy family. The only death was a peaceful one. Doesn't fit your usual profile of a haunting."

Despite her nerves, Anjali was intrigued. "Is there a typical haunting?"

"Basically, there are three categories. You have your residual haunting, where the spirit or ghost is seen repeating the same action over and over. You have your interactive spirit, where the presence actually interacts with the inhabitants, slamming doors, weird noises. The spirit is as aware of you as you are of it. And then the third . . ." He paused.

An icy breeze kissed the nape of her neck. Anjali did not need to turn to know all the windows were closed. The cold wasn't coming from outside. The cold was generated from the thought in Scott's head.

"The third category is an entity," he said in a matter-of-fact voice. "A nonhuman presence, ancient and ageless. Sometimes referred to as a demon or demonic presence. It's debatable whether or not poltergeists fit into this category. I think they border between interactive spirits and entities."

Anjali strove for his no-nonsense tone but didn't quite succeed. "Have you ever encountered an entity?"

"No. And I hope I never do. Although from a purely intellectual standpoint—"

"Can we get this over with?"

Scott checked his watch. "Ten to eight. It's about a thirty-minute drive. Let's go. Ready?"

"Like hell."

13

A bar brawl was too risky.

Too many people, and there was the risk of the police being called.

Coulter hadn't contacted Rachel since her crazy, gun-toting, ex-girlfriend had tried to kill him.

Instead he was out for a night stroll through the Tenderloin district, supposedly the sketchiest neighborhood in San Francisco. Coulter had been disappointed. The area seemed nice. He'd walked by crowded ethnic restaurants and colorful dive bars.

Annoyed, he was ready to return to his cheap motel. Apparently the streets were a lot safer than they used to be.

But as the hour grew late, he ventured deep into the darker parts, sidestepping panhandlers, tipping his hat to prostitutes, and stepping on at least a half-dozen syringes.

The air grew thick with menace. Just what Coulter was looking for.

He was asking for it.

Literally.

He needed money, and he needed to practice his new-found skill. That's why he was walking around San Francisco in the middle of the night, trying to look like a hick who didn't know any better.

Finally he heard the sound of footsteps creeping up on him. Come on, he thought. He walked faster, and the footsteps also sped up.

All of a sudden the collar of his denim jacket was grabbed from behind.

"Your wallet. Now." The voice was young, male, and tough.

Coulter had to stop himself from smiling.

He turned around. The mugger was wearing a ski mask and a fatigue jacket. And for the second time in days a gun was pointed at him, this time a little higher up at the chest.

"I reckon I'm gonna need my money," he said, heavy on the drawl. "San Francisco's an expensive city. That okay with you?"

The mugger's hand on the gun was steady. "Don't mess with me, cowboy, hand over the money."

"I don't know. This wallet here belonged to my grand-daddy."

"I'll kill you and take it anyway. You think I won't?"

"If I thought that I wouldn't be here."

This was it. Show time. Coulter concentrated on the mugger.

Nothing happened.

Shit!

The mugger's hand tightened on the trigger. "All right, Kid Rock, time's up."

Coulter could feel a small bead of panic sliding down his back.

What a goddamn bullshit way to die.

He was psychic. Not Superman.

He was working up to full panic mode when it happened.

The pull in his gut, and the mugger went flying back into a pile of trash bags. The plastic burst at the seams, and rank refuse spilled all over.

"Thank you, Jesus!" Coulter kicked the gun into the sewer drain and slowly approached the man on the ground.

The mugger's eyes behind the mask were wide. Shakily, he held out his wallet. Coulter took it, emptied it of cash, and tossed it back. "I hope you appreciate the irony of this moment, my friend. *I'm* mugging *you*."

He headed back to the motel.

Only this time he was whistling.

14

Anjali stared at the house and felt her stomach clench. She should never have come here. She should never have left her safe, secure apartment.

"Hey," Scott said, "remember what I told you."

They were sitting in his black Range Rover staring out at the house.

"I'm supposed to guide whatever is in there toward the light. I sound like a Hollywood cliché."

Scott tapped his fingers on the steering wheel. "Some people believe that when you die there is a wonderful light. All the answers to all the questions you want to know are there. And when you walk to it . . . you become a part of that energy forever."

"But some people die, and they don't know they're gone," she said.

"For some reason they resist going into the light. And then some people just get lost on the way there. They need someone to lead them. That's where you come in."

Anjali frowned. "You're not making all this up, are you?"

"I can't tell you why you've been given this particular ability; no one can," Scott said gently. "All I know is that spirits can keep themselves from moving on if their will is strong enough. But if my assessment of your ability is correct, your will is stronger. Just close your eyes and focus as if you were meditating."

"Meditation, huh?" Anjali raised an eyebrow. "You know that was invented in India."

"Yes."

"So was chess."

"I'd read that somewhere."

"And dice."

"Dice?"

"And hippies. A lost tribe of fair-skinned people who were forced out of India and relocated to America where they lived freely wearing love beads, playing the sitar, and totally getting into Indian spirituality."

"I see."

"And yoga. But not Hare Krishnas. Shaved heads and begging in airports have never been what India's about."

He smiled. "Oh yeah?"

"And pasta."

"I believe that was invented in China."

"Close enough."

"Ready to take a look at the house?"

"No." But she opened the car door and stepped out.

She started up the drive, but the sound of a car pulling

up made her turn around. An old Honda Civic parked in the driveway. Lynne Michaels was home.

Scott held the car door open for her. "Lynne, there's someone I'd like you to meet. This is Anjali."

Lynne turned to her with a small, tight smile. Her hair was pulled back in a ponytail. She wore no makeup. "So you're the psychic?"

Anjali was totally embarrassed. "That's me. Got any spoons to bend?"

Nobody laughed.

"The kids are at a neighbor's," Lynne said. "Come on in."

Anjali reached under her shirt and pulled out her Ganesh pendant so the delicate chain rested above the neckline of her red tee. Her mother had given her the necklace for her sixteenth birthday. The feel of it against her skin was somehow reassuring.

Scott reached out and lightly touched the chain. "That's nice. Ganesh?"

"It's said that if you give Ganesh your love and energy, he will reward you and remove all the obstacles in your life. But if you ignore him, destruction will rain down on you with the force of a hundred elephants."

"Good to know."

Ahead of them, Lynne waited beside the open front door. Anjali took a deep breath and walked toward her. *I'm protected,* she thought. *I've learned how to block. I can do this.*

She crossed the threshold.

There was definitely a presence in the house. She knew it as certainly as if she'd been able to hear or see it.

No alien thoughts or emotions struggled to breach the barrier of her mind. Instead, it was like being in one part of the house and hearing the faucet running in the kitchen. Simply an awareness, neither good nor bad.

The knot in her stomach relaxed a bit, and she was able to focus. She could feel Scott's expectations, his certainty that she would discover something. Lynne's interest tinged with skepticism. She pushed those feelings aside. The room came to her then. Weak wisps of emotion, happiness, tranquillity, some sadness. Nothing lingered.

"I'm barely getting anything here," she said. She tried to keep the relief out of her voice. She didn't think she succeeded.

They visited each and every room on the first and second floor and some very nonspooky bathrooms. Nothing dramatic had happened on the toilet or in the bath. Attics were supposed to house spooks, and this one even had cobwebs and enough shadows to make any ghoul feel at home, but Anjali didn't encounter the presence.

"I don't know what else to show you," Lynne said helplessly.

Anjali headed back toward the family room. There was one more area they hadn't explored. She stopped in front of a door just off the main room. "This leads to the garage, doesn't it?"

"What are you sensing?" Scott asked, pulling out a small rectangular machine.

He'd told her it was an EMF meter. He'd tried to explain what it did, but quantum mechanics had never been her strength. She could spell *electromagnetic* and that was about it.

"I feel like there's something on the other side of this door," Anjali said. "Why would any spirit choose to haunt a garage?"

Amused, Scott looked at her. "There's always a first time."

"What does your gadget tell you?"

"Something is definitely there."

"The water heater started leaking the first week we moved in," Lynne said. "So I've been parking the car outside."

Anjali turned the door handle, but the door wouldn't budge. "It's stuck."

"The spirit could be holding it shut," Scott said.

"Umm, I think it's just locked, guys." Lynne reached out and twisted the bolt. The door opened.

Anjali looked at Scott. They exchanged sheepish glances. Shaking her head, she went inside.

The force of emotion hit her like a tidal wave, nearly knocking her down.

The room filled her up. Swallowed her whole. Everything was cold.

"Anjali?" She could hear Scott calling her as if from a distance.

Her instinct was to run, get out, but then she felt his hand on her shoulder, firm and strong. And she realized she was still standing. She was still breathing.

"I'm okay," she said. "The shock of it . . . hit me."

Scott gazed at her with concern. "Are you sure? Do you want to go outside?"

Lynne's face was pale and drawn. "You went still all of a sudden. Your body became so stiff."

Feeling as if she had to put on a brave front (even though she wanted to go screaming into the night), Anjali smiled. "That couldn't have been very attractive."

She turned to Scott. "The presence is male. I don't sense anything mean or violent. But for the life of me I can't figure out what he wants."

"Take a deep breath," Scott said. "And close your eyes. Now what do you see?"

"It's all jumbled. Cabinets. Tools? Power tools?" In the past, Anjali would have left a haunted locale by this point. Now she focused hard. Dug deep. Trying to understand the images and thoughts in her head. She saw a half-finished birdhouse resting on a wooden table. "This was his room," she said. "He worked here. He loved his projects."

"I wonder," Scott began, "if the leaking water, the missing tools, the noises at night, are more of his projects? Part of his existence, between this world and the next?"

Anjali sighed. "I never thought I'd grow up to be a therapist for dead people."

"Will he leave?" Lynne asked quietly. "I know this was his house, but can you please make him leave?"

Anjali looked at Scott. "What do I do?"

Scott's gaze did not waver from hers. "Visualize a doorway filled with light. Urge him toward it. Tell him about his family. Make him aware it's time to move on."

Anjali took a few steps deeper into the room and started closing her eyes.

"Wait!" Scott said. He was holding the digital camera. "I need to put this on video mode."

Anjali let out a sigh of impatience but held off freeing the tormented spirit until he gave her a thumbs-up.

She closed her eyes and envisioned a doorway spilling with light. She guided the spirit toward it, mentally telling him about his family, how his wife had moved. It was time for him to go.

She hoped he was listening.

There was a long, drawn-out sigh, and the room grew warmer.

"This house is clean," she said.

And it was. She couldn't feel anything anymore.

Scott came to her, eyes shining. "He's gone. You did it." He pulled her into a hug.

"The air shimmered," Lynne said. "I saw something or I think I saw something, but the house feels different. You really did it."

"I think—" Anjali began, and fainted in Scott's arms.

15

$\int$ cott didn't expect another case to fall into his lap so soon.

He'd just had lunch with Kyle Chang, his roommate from Stanford. Kyle's mom was a Realtor in the Bay Area and was being sued by the buyers of a new home for selling them a property infested with spirits.

Not as far-fetched as one would think.

Recently, California legislators had pushed through a bill making it mandatory for all home sellers to disclose any supernatural phenomena related to the property.

Driving home, Scott realized he should be elated.

He wasn't.

Anjali was gone.

But he'd made a deal. Just one case, and he'd never bother her again. Scott did not go back on his word.

Something they hadn't taught him in business school.

And even if he did find a true psychic willing to work with him, there was no guarantee he or she would have Anjali's ability.

He'd been astounded by what she'd accomplished at Lynne Michaels's home and that his theory—guiding spirits to awareness, visualized as a doorway filled with light— was correct. Anjali had made contact. She'd communicated with the dead.

And the dead had listened.

Scott's one desire was to make contact with the spirit world. To interact with someone from the other side. And Anjali had brought him closer than he ever thought possible.

He was so caught up with thoughts of the spirit world that he wasn't paying much attention to Earth. He nearly hit the Buick turning left in front of him.

The old man stuck his fist out the window and gave Scott the finger. "Ass wipe!"

Scott might have dedicated his life to investigating ghosts, but he wasn't ready to become one just yet. He followed the rules of the road, and fifteen minutes later pulled into the detached garage behind his house.

Intent on picking up his mail, he circled the house to the front.

"Counselor Troi was the most useless crew member on the *Enterprise*," Anjali said by way of greeting.

Startled, Scott turned around. She was sitting on his front steps, clad in jeans and a black turtleneck, arms wrapped around her drawn-up legs.

"Counselor Troi?" he said.

Anjali imitated the character. "I sense anger, Captain . . .

well, duh! The Romulans have once again threatened to destroy the ship. When haven't the Romulans been angry?"

Scott tried not to look too hopeful as he approached her. "In a contest of empaths you could have kicked the crap out of Counselor Troi."

She smiled. "Did I tell you I once went to the local precinct to offer my services as a psychic?"

He was surprised. "No."

"I was thirteen. Well before the Bradford House incident. And I had the crazy idea that I could help the police solve crimes or find missing people."

He was pretty sure of the outcome of her visit but asked anyway. "What happened?"

"I was laughed out of the station. As I ran off, one of the sergeants called out 'We've already got Nostradamus on the payroll, sweetheart.' It was humiliating. Although looking back, I can't really blame them for their reaction."

Hope began to build inside him. He started to tell her about his friend, a detective with the SFPD who would welcome her unique talent on a case, but he kept his mouth shut and waited for her to finish.

"The morning after the Michaels . . . house cleaning, I woke up feeling different. Like I'd accomplished something. Like I really helped someone. I've never felt that way before." She gave a short laugh. "I don't know what that says about me as a human being."

He thought she was being too hard on herself, but they'd discuss her self-esteem issues later. "Are you saying what I think you're saying?"

She tucked a lock of long black hair behind her ear and

stood up. "The next time you need help on a case, I'm available."

He smiled. "Great. Let's get started."

"Now?"

"Got the call this morning."

She tilted her head to the side and looked at him. "This is a nonprofit firm, isn't it? You do this free of charge?"

"Yes, but we can work out a salary, something on a case-by-case basis."

He was surprised when she laughed.

"I worked at a job I hated for the money and the stock options. I don't want this to be about money. I want it to be about purpose. Besides"—a glint came into her eyes— "you couldn't afford me anyway."

Scott was amused and a little touched. He wasn't about to go into his trust fund and stakes in various Wilder corporations. "You're doing this for your karma."

Anjali shrugged. "You could say that. Destiny doesn't do dental plans."

16

The medical director of the Oakland Imaging Facility was an old friend of Vivica's.

Vivica used the word *friend* loosely.

In actuality, she'd slept with the man years ago. Now, in return for one session with the facility's FMRI machine, she promised not to tell his wife about the affair.

Vivica used the word *affair* loosely.

They had sex once and she'd yawned her way through half of it.

Normally, an MRI machine was the best method for studying the brain. But the new Functional MRI actually created movies of brain activity by precisely tracking the flow of blood and putting several images together. An FMRI scan provided maps of the brain in outstanding detail. Maps that could then be correlated with different mental processes.

Like psychic activity.

After thirty minutes in the interior of the machine, Hans Morden now lay supine on a table outside of it.

Vivica stared at the results displayed on the computer screen. Rarely taken by surprise, she found herself stunned. "I've never seen anything like this," she murmured.

Gaspar and Fitch hovered nearby at attention. "Seen what?" Gasper asked.

"This readout matches the ones done on telekinetics and telepaths. It's almost as if . . ."

"What?" Fitch demanded. "What?"

Vivica straightened. "Never mind. I—I'm not sure." She quickly printed out the readout and hit record for the results to be saved on DVD as well.

"Why is he in a trance?" Gaspar asked.

Vivica frowned. "I don't know. He goes into these fugue states on his own. I don't like it. He becomes unreachable."

"Well, so far I haven't seen Hans do anything amazing," Fitch said. "He never talks. Most of the time he just sits there staring off into space. Are you sure he's not retarded?"

Suddenly the pile of folders next to Fitch burst into flame. He gasped and stumbled back.

Gaspar grabbed the fire extinguisher and put it out.

Vivica arched a brow. "Did I forget to mention Hans is a pyrokinetic?"

The door opened then and Maddox walked in, a newspaper tucked under his arm.

"There's something in here you should see." He laid the paper in front of Vivica. The *San Francisco Chronicle* was folded to the last page. A small paragraph was circled in red.

"Hey," Gaspar said. "You just missed Fitch nearly getting barbecued."

"Quiet!" Vivica read the few lines in a matter of seconds. She looked up. "That's all the information they have?"

"I spoke to my source," Maddox said. "This woman, Rachel, claims that without touching the assailant, he made her fly back and hit the wall."

"A telekinetic," Vivica said thoughtfully. "But they don't have a name or address?"

"They have a name. The reporter just wasn't allowed to print it. Coulter Marshall."

"The three of you get on it. Convince this Coulter to come in."

After the trio left, Vivica walked back to the machine and knelt so she was eye level with Hans. "Nice display, Mr. Morden."

The man stared at the ceiling unsmiling.

"There's something very interesting about you. Most psychics have one defined ability: telekinesis, telepathy, pyrokinesis, but you . . . you have all of the above."

She leaned closer. "You're going to make me very famous."

17

"**W**elcome to 1313 Mockingbird Lane," Scott said.

Anjali stepped out of his car, double-checked that the gold Ganesh pendant was around her neck, and surveyed the dwelling in front of her. Even in the unusually warm Northern California sunshine, the gloomy house sagged with depressive weight.

"Hey," Scott said. With a smile he cocked his head to the house next door. "That's our house."

Anjali saw a neatly tended, snug, two-story house with rows of daffodils and a magnolia tree in the front yard.

Don't judge a haunted house by its exterior, she thought.

Relief mixed with anger swept through her. "You're an asshole, Wilder."

He grinned. "So you tell me. Let's get to work."

Rosie Chang, the Realtor, stood in front of the house

waiting for them. In her mid-fifties, dressed in a well-cut powder pink suit and a string of pearls, she exuded confidence and surveyed Anjali with a critical eye. "You look Indian."

"I am."

"Married?"

"Single."

"You do this full-time? Or you have real career?"

"Neither, I guess."

Rosie shook her head. "You first-generation Americans are confused people. My daughter thinks she's Britney Spears. Dyes her black hair blond."

Anjali supposed *confused* was one way to look at it. She preferred to think of herself as *complex*. She was a Hindu who ate beef and a cynic who communicated with the dead.

Yeehaw!

"Let's take a look at the house," Scott said.

Anjali followed the other two inside. Crossing the threshold, she held her breath.

Scott looked at her. "Getting anything?"

"Not yet."

"See!" Rosie stomped her foot. "No ghosts in this damn house!"

"What's that smell?" Scott wrinkled his nose as they entered the hall.

"Chinese herbs," Rose answered. "Good for feng shui."

Anjali reflected that if you built your house on a burial ground—as some developers blindly tended to do—you could feng shui the hell out of the place and it wasn't going to make a difference.

Still, she liked the smell. "Reminds me of mint chutney."

Anjali and Scott checked out the first floor, walking from the family room to the kitchen and then back to the entrance hall, where Rosie waited with her hands on her hips and a scowl on her face. "This house worth $750,000. Stupid ghosts bad for business!"

"I'm barely getting anything down here," Anjali said.

Rosie scowled. "That's what I say! Stupid owners on drugs."

From upstairs came the sharp sound of a door being slammed.

"Master bedroom," Rosie said. "Door won't stay open."

"Is that right?" Scott asked. "Possible interactive spirit."

Anjali tucked her thumbs into the waist of her jeans and gazed up at the second floor landing. There was something there. She was starting to feel it. "I sense someone now, a female presence. The previous owner of the house?"

Rosie's cell phone rang. She snapped it open and spoke rapidly in Chinese for a moment before hanging up. "Broker keeps calling. Wants to know what's happening. I told him—drink green tea and chill."

"Don't worry," Anjali said. "I've done a procedure like this before." She caught Scott's eye and smiled.

Scott turned on the camera. "Upstairs?"

"After you," she said and started up, looking back as Rosie followed. "You might be more comfortable waiting downstairs."

Rosie leveled her with a steely gaze. "Every year someone try to sabotage my sales. Last year it was Connie Wang, now it's ghost bitch. I'm going."

As they went up Anjali trailed her fingers along the

smooth wooden banister, picking up images and emotions along the way. Fleeting glimpses of all the living beings who'd ever dwelled in the house.

They reached the master bedroom. "It's going to be cold," Scott warned Rosie.

"Oh," she said. "Just like in *The Sixth Sense*."

Anjali counted to three, opened the door, and stepped into the room.

The cold surrounded them, seeping through their clothes, sliding down their throats. The very definition of bone-chilling. They'd found the heart of the house.

Scott and Anjali were prepared, but beside them, Rosie shivered and looked uneasy. Anjali reached out and put a hand on her shoulder.

Scott aimed the EMF meter around the room. Anjali watched him. "What are you doing? I think we've determined this place is haunted already."

"The readings will be transferred into my laptop as proof," he said and added in a dry voice. "Remember skeptics?"

Behind them the door slammed shut.

Rosie jumped. "*Chiu!*"

"That's okay," Anjali said, trying for a calm voice. "That's about the most she can do."

"Are you sure?"

This presence was definitely not that of a kindly old man tinkering in his garage.

"Positive," she lied.

Scott gave her an encouraging smile. "Ghosts don't kill people. Running away from ghosts, tripping and breaking your neck in the process, kills people."

"Right," she said.

He pulled out the video camera from his bag.

Anjali squared her shoulders and got to work.

She walked out to the middle of the empty room, her footsteps sounding abnormally loud against the hardwood floor. Touching her Ganesh again, she closed her eyes and reached out with her mind.

The male presence in the Michaels house had left on his own after she'd nudged him toward the fact he was dead. So she tried that again.

Nothing.

"It's not working Scott."

"Ask her if she has a message for the living."

Is there anything you want to tell me?

Instead of cooperating, the female presence filled Anjali's mind with visions: Rosie screaming her name. The walls of the house shaking and crumbling. Scott lying on the floor twisting in agony.

The presence was trying to scare her and overdoing it in Anjali's opinion. Still, it was working.

Spectral fingers danced along the back of her neck.

She wanted to turn around, wanted to see, but stayed in place, her eyes closed. Focusing, tuning out everything else.

Once again, she reached out and explained to the presence that she needed to leave, her time was over. She visualized the doorway filled with light and urged the spirit toward it.

The spirit refused to budge.

Ghostly laughter filled the room.

Anjali's fear was slowly replaced by annoyance.

She recalled what Scott had said. Spirits could keep themselves from moving on if their will was strong enough.

But Anjali's will was stronger.

She focused hard on the doorway filled with light and guided—okay, willed—okay, shoved—the spirit toward it.

Concentrating, all it took was one final mental push, and the spirit slipped out of this world.

The air around them grew warmer.

She opened her eyes. "This house is clean."

Rosie was wide-eyed, her hands pressed to her chest. "Oh boy! Oh boy! You did it!"

Scott stared at her, the hand with the camera drifting down to his leg. "Amazing. I still can't believe this works."

Rosie tilted her head and looked at Anjali. "You should still find real career though. No money in this ghost-busting stuff."

18

During a brief stint in Texas, Coulter had romanced a preacher's daughter who taught him two things.

One, God loves you.

Two, you're going to hell.

He thought of what she'd said as he started a new career. Strolling the streets of San Francisco after dark, targeting criminals by making himself a target and depriving them of their hard-earned dollars.

On one hand, God had to love him because Coulter was using the talent the Divine Father had given him.

On the other, Coulter Marshall was destined for hell as surely as a bored housewife was sitting down to watch *The Price Is Right*.

His new racket proved it.

Until that day of reckoning though, he was going to enjoy

himself. Number one on his list—check out of the cockroach castle he'd been staying in since he got to the city. Bugs in the bathroom, porn in the magazine rack, and bedsheets that hadn't been washed since Velcro was invented.

The location wasn't too desirable either, situated as it was between the Church of Satan and the Temple of Uranus—a bathhouse exclusively for men.

And no, Coulter had not taken a dip.

He was just heading out, pushing through the grimy door when a dark SUV screeched to the curb, techno music blasting, and three men who looked like extras from *Men in Black* spilled out.

"This place is a dump," one of them said, staring up at the motel.

His companion sneered. "What was your first clue? The hookers in the lobby?"

"Can we get on with it?" the third one said. "Vivica doesn't want us taking all day."

Coulter stood aside to let them pass. They barely glanced at him.

He walked to the end of the block, and then caught the uptown bus. He was going to treat himself. Three-star hotel all the way.

19

"**S**he cursed me," Fitch whispered.

Maddox frowned. "Will you shut it?"

"I think she did curse him," Gaspar murmured. "My Spanish is rusty but I swear it had something to do with Fitch's manly parts."

"Silence!" Veda commanded.

After missing Coulter at his motel, Gaspar, Maddox, and Fitch were at The Magic Wand, Veda's small magic shop on Haight. Veda was supposedly a witch, and Maddox thought she fit the bill. She had long silver hair, a hooked nose, and eyes that seemed to pierce right through them.

According to Vivica, Veda possessed a weak but true second sight, and her specialty was divining.

Maddox thought another one of Veda's specialties was marketing. Tarot cards, candles, and charms filled the shelves, and judging by the silver Mercedes parked outside, business was good.

"The name!" Veda barked.

"Coulter Marshall," Maddox supplied.

Fitch nudged Gaspar. "Wonder why she needs a Benz when a broomstick would beat traffic?" The two men snickered.

Maddox leaned toward them. "Do you want to keep making jokes or do you want to find this guy? Hmm . . . what option would Vivica prefer?"

Fitch and Gaspar settled back in their seats with various expressions of annoyance and fear. But they were quiet.

"Now." Veda beamed. "Let me look into my crystal ball."

It was too much. Even Maddox began snickering.

Veda looked up. "There is too much negative interference. I can't see anything."

Fitch coughed into his hand. "Fraud."

"Anyone smell snake oil?" Gaspar questioned.

Maddox pulled out a fifty-dollar bill. "If you want us to cross your palm with silver, lady, I'm going to need more."

Veda frowned and returned to her crystal ball. "I see sawdust on the floor. Dancing. Not too far from here." She threw up her hands. "Nothing else. My head pains me. Leave."

"Country-western bar," Maddox said.

Gaspar pulled out his cell phone. "I'll get a list of all the potentials in the area."

"Let's go." Fitch rose. "I think she gave me hives."

"You're too impressionable." Maddox tossed the money on the table, and the three men walked out.

*   *   *

Veda glared at their backs.

The crystal ball was just for effect. As soon as she'd been given the details, a location had formed in her mind. A place she knew well.

The Rockin' Rodeo on Fulton.

Thursday was Ladies' Night.

But she didn't tell Vivica's men that. She pocketed the money. "Dumbshits," she muttered.

20

So a psychic and a ghost hunter walk into a bar.

Anjali stared warily at the man in a Confederate flag shirt exiting the Rockin' Rodeo. She turned to Scott. "I think I'm too brown to feel comfortable in there. You know me and my redneck phobia."

With his hand on her waist, he steered her through the entrance. "We're in San Francisco. How red can their necks be?"

"You obviously didn't see *48 Hours*. Eddie Murphy walks into a country-western bar in San Francisco and the whole room screeches to a halt."

"Don't worry," Scott said.

The sawdust crunched under her feet, she didn't recognize what was playing on the jukebox, and everyone had a domestic beer in his hand.

Anjali didn't feel very comforted.

Besides, how was she supposed to recognize this Coulter person anyway? There were a dozen blond-haired, blue-eyed men in the place. "Didn't your friend Eddie have any other details about our guy?"

"All he knows is that Vivica's lapdogs have checked out every Western dive in the city, save this one and the Sundance Saloon. If we strike out here, we'll head there next. Once Vivica gets her hands on this Coulter guy, I won't be able to get within one foot of him. And the chance to talk to an actual telekinetic? I have so many questions!"

Anjali stared at him. He was practically glowing with excitement.

He's like a kid in a clairvoyant candy store, she thought.

He maneuvered her toward the bar. "See if you can pick up anything."

"I'll try."

Scott ordered two Millers and asked the bartender if he knew of a Coulter Marshall.

"Nope." The bartender uncapped two bottles and set them on the counter. "Five bucks." He turned away to take another order.

Anjali noticed the woman in a halter top and tight jeans seated on a bar stool next to them. She knew something about Coulter. Anjali couldn't sense any information beyond that, but did notice the woman's eyes sliding over Scott.

With one hand on his back, Anjali reached for her beer and dropped her voice to a whisper. "Talk to Ms. Halter Top next to you. She knows something and thinks you're cute."

"And what will you do?"

"Investigate."

She cut through the crowd and went to stand by the jukebox, scanning the titles. The next song cued up was by someone named Alison Krauss. She looked back to see Scott and the brunette deep in conversation.

Unsure of how exactly to go about investigating, she remained by the jukebox and tried to look like she belonged. She certainly stood out. Didn't minorities go country line dancing? Or maybe she was being unnecessarily self-conscious.

After fifteen minutes she hadn't picked up anything. But she'd become a fan of Alison Krauss and Gretchen Wilson.

Sipping on her beer she sat down on a bar stool at the opposite end of the bar from Scott and decided to people watch.

Since Anjali had started working as a psychic, actively using her abilities instead of trying to stifle them, she felt less like a victim and more in control of her life. She even contemplated writing a book. And inspired by the Rockin' Rodeo, she'd come up with a title.

Even Mediums Get the Blues.

She was distracted from her literary musings (which included being an Oprah's Book Club pick) by a couple on the dance floor.

The plump blond had her arms wrapped around her date's muscular neck as they ground their lips and hips against each other, oblivious to all the people around them.

Meanwhile, the only guy paying attention to Anjali was the bald man with a beer belly hanging over his Bronco buckle, breathing all over her.

Across the room, Halter Top had her hand on Scott's

shoulder, and he was laughing, leaning in close to her. Anjali scowled. How long did it take to elicit information anyway?

A giggle caught her attention, and Anjali turned to see the horny humping couple walking by her. The man's arm brushed against her shoulder, and Anjali felt as though the wind had been knocked out of her.

His feelings came through dark and strong.

He was dangerous.

Perverse.

The woman was in trouble.

The couple headed out the back exit. Sliding off the stool, as if on automatic pilot, she followed them.

Anjali trailed the pair into a dark alley.

Now what? she thought.

They were directly in front of her. She had to do something. If she ran to get help, she'd lose them.

So she did the only thing a female with no martial arts training could do.

She threw back her head and screamed.

The couple whirled around and stared at her.

Anjali took a step toward the blond. "Don't go with him," she blurted. "He's a sex criminal!"

She didn't know what else to call him. Mr. Pervert seemed too lenient. Rapist was a possibility but she didn't really know what his intentions were, just his depraved feelings behind them.

"Is she crazy or what?" Blond asked.

"Probably drunk," Sex Criminal said smoothly.

Anjali made eye contact with the woman. "You have to

believe me. The man you're with is violent. You can't leave with him."

Sex Criminal tugged on his date's arm. "Let's get out of here."

Anjali focused on the blond, opening her mind to the other woman's thoughts. "I know you just met him. You think he's the one. You think he's saved you from a string of Saturday nights spent with Häagen-Dazs and chick flicks. You've watched *Cocktail* so many times, you know the dialogue by heart. Which I can't understand because although I liked the movie when I saw it the first time in high school, I saw it again years later and it really sucked."

The woman's eyes widened. "How . . ." She looked at the man beside her, then back at Anjali. "I . . . I need to get out of here."

Anjali watched her go off with a sigh of relief.

Then she realized she was now alone in a dark alley with a sexual deviant.

She took a step backward, intending to break into a run.

He lunged, grabbing her arm and twisting it hard, dragging her toward him.

"I don't know who you are, but you made a big mistake, sweetness."

He began dragging her toward the end of the alley, his grip unbreakable.

"Now that's no way to treat a lady," a male voice purred from the darkness.

Sex Criminal's fingers dug painfully into the soft flesh of her upper arm. "Stay out of this. It's none of your business."

"Yes it is," Anjali called out and winced as the bruising grip tightened on her arm.

As the stranger approached them, her skin began to tingle and tighten. There was now a crackle to the air, the sizzling charge of static electricity.

The stranger was the source. Anjali knew this as certainly as she knew the words to every Depeche Mode song ever written.

The man cruelly gripping her arm, however, seemed to be oblivious to the electrical current slicing through the air. That or he was too occupied with thoughts of a criminally sexual nature. "Leave. This doesn't concern you," he said.

The stranger's lean form drew closer. "Well, there are things I don't consider my concern. Politics for one. Proper etiquette for another. And what is or isn't corrupting the tender youth of America today. But a cock monster like you . . . concerns me."

Anjali was shoved out of the way as her would-be attacker charged and caught the stranger around the middle, pinning his arms to his sides.

The stranger struggled, trying to break the stronger man's grip.

Desperate, Anjali looked around for someone to call, some way to help, when the Sex Criminal abruptly released the stranger and staggered back as if pushed. A look of astonishment passed over his face before he went flying back. His body slammed against the brick wall and crumpled to the pavement.

Anjali blinked, trying to process what she'd just seen.

The stranger walked forward into a dimly lit patch of light. Anjali blinked several more times and tried not to gape. She did not succeed.

Her rescuer had blond hair, blue eyes, and a face so perfect it was devastating.

Holy shit, the man was testosterone on two legs.

"Thank you," she said, continuing to stare.

"De nada, sweetheart." He leaned over and searched the limp man's body, pulling out his wallet. Grabbing a wad of bills, he stuffed them into his pocket.

"Word of warning," he said. "You can tell people about what you saw tonight, but you'll come off looking crazier than a faith healer at a revival meeting."

He started to walk away, and Anjali finally found her voice. "Wait! Coulter!"

He stopped and glanced over his shoulder.

She took a deep breath. "I'm psychic too."

He walked back, stood in front of her, and gazed down at her face. "Well now." He smiled. "Isn't that interesting?"

The noise inside the bar had risen to extreme levels.

Anjali saw a giant in a wife-beater advancing on three men dressed in identical dark suits. "Which one of you stiffs called me a hick?"

Ignoring them, she walked up to Scott, overhearing him ask the brunette next to him, "So you think Coulter will come in tonight?"

"Pretty sure," she said, her gaze warm with invitation. "Now, about your number?"

Anjali tapped Scott on the shoulder. He turned, and she gestured to the man beside her. "I'd like you to meet Mr. Marshall."

21

Scott hit stop on the TV remote, and the footage of the Chang case disappeared. "So what do you think?"

Coulter yawned and stretched his arms so they rested along the back of the sofa. "Could have used a soundtrack."

"Besides that," Scott said.

"I can't believe you guys go after ghosts and spirits and all that Halloween stuff."

"It's about the search for truth," Scott said.

Coulter grinned. "Okay, Mulder."

Anjali giggled.

Coulter looked her up and down, his gaze appreciative. "How do you say your name again?"

"Un-ja-lee."

"I'll just call you Angel."

She giggled again.

Scott rolled his eyes. The three of them had gathered in the den after coming straight from the Rockin' Rodeo. He'd been eager to quiz Coulter about his abilities but decided to show him the recordings from the Lynne Michaels and Rosie Chang cases. To demonstrate what The Cold Spot: Paranormal Investigations was all about.

"So," Scott said. "Any other thoughts? Questions about the firm?"

"Just one," Coulter said. "Isn't The Cold Spot 7-Up's logo?"

"Oh my God!" Anjali exclaimed. "It is!"

Scott rubbed the space between his eyebrows where he most often developed a headache. "Besides being a soft drink, The Cold Spot also refers to an area of psychic energy, relating to a spirit or entity."

"Speaking of spirits," Coulter said. "Got any whiskey?"

"Drinks. Right." In automatic host mode, he went to the bar and poured a vodka tonic, handing it to Anjali without her asking.

"I'm impressed," she said. "How'd you know my drink?"

He smiled. "You hang around with psychics long enough . . ."

Instead of whiskey, he offered Coulter an alternative. "Try this. I'm partial to it myself."

Coulter took a sip and groaned, closing his eyes. "I think I see Jesus. What is this?"

"Single malt Scotch."

Scott declined to take a drink for himself and leaned against the bar. "Do you have any idea where your powers came from?"

Coulter waved the Scotch under his nose. "Off the back of a cereal box?"

Scott continued to study him. Coulter looked up and with a resigned shrug, set his glass aside.

"I know nothing about the good ol' family tree. Hell, I don't even know who my daddy is."

Scott had to ask. "Ever have a near death experience?"

A lazy smile spread across Coulter's face. "Well now, the Grim Reaper and I are good friends, text each other on a regular basis like a couple of teenage girls. But I've never walked into the light—if that's what you mean."

"What about a blow to the head?" Anjali asked. She looked at Scott. "Do blows to the head really cause psychic ability?"

"If that were true, Mike Tyson would be channeling spirits in the ring." Scott pushed himself away from the bar and walked to the center of the room. "So you don't know where or how your abilities originated. That's fine. Anjali's not too sure of hers either."

"And I've got my family tree traced back for generations." She frowned. "I'm not sure how accurate the information is though. I don't think I'm a direct descendant of both Buddha and Gandhi."

"What would be interesting," Scott said, "is seeing if your children and your grandchildren inherit your ESP."

"If that happens," Anjali said angrily, "I definitely won't make them feel like science experiments because of it."

Coulter gave her a speculative look. "I think the first words I learned to say were *demon* and *spawn*, seeing as how my mama said them to me often enough."

"So you also grew up feeling like there was something wrong with you?" Anjali asked.

Coulter looked surprised. "Not at all. I felt pretty superior actually." He looked at Scott. "Hey Spock, what's your thing? What can you do?"

Scott saw Anjali trying to hide a smile.

He cleared his throat. "Nothing actually. I'm not psychic." The topic was a sore spot for him. He would give anything to touch the other side, to fully experience it as someone other than an observer.

"Well, are ya'll gonna ask me or what?" Coulter said.

Scott and Anjali looked at him.

Coulter stood up. "For a demonstration? I'll start with a little spoon bending."

Coulter bent spoons, bent them back into shape, made them dance in the air, and then moved on to dishware.

Scott stood in front of Coulter, the EMF meter raised and pointed.

"What is that thing?" Coulter asked.

Scott stared at the readings. "Just what I thought! The amount of energy you're giving off is incredible!"

Anjali crossed to his side. "I couldn't tell an electromagnetic wave from a sound wave but the meter is definitely getting excited."

"Now this is just my opinion," Scott began (and since his opinion had been quoted in a well-known scientific journal, he believed it held sufficient weight). "Coulter is absorbing the electrical energy from the air around him. He's soaking it up . . . storing it if you will. I'm sure he does this even when he's sleeping."

Anjali smiled at him. "You energy hog."

Scott took a few more readings, then plugged the meter into his iPAQ PDA, storing the data. He turned around just as a plate swept through the air and stopped barely an inch from his face, making him flinch. Several more plates circled around his head. "Very nice," he said in a flat voice. "Can we move on?"

Flying objects landed safely on the coffee table, and Coulter sat back down on the sofa.

Demonstration over, Scott got down to business and addressed Coulter. "What I want to do is put you in—for lack of a better word—a haunted house and see what happens, see how the house reacts to you and how you react to it."

"See what the spirits make of him?" Anjali asked.

"Exactly."

Coulter leaned back, resting his foot on his thigh. "Sounds easy enough to me. How much you payin'?"

"First let me say that this is a nonprofit business. People would be less inclined to seek out our help if we charged."

"You're doin' this for free? Ever hear of doctors? They help people too and don't bat an eye when it comes to their fee."

Scott sought to explain. "For me, it's not about the money—"

Coulter swept his hand in indication of the flat-panel TV, the leather sofa and chairs. "People who have money always say that."

Scott was in no mood to justify his business practices. "The amount I'm offering," he began just as Anjali stood up.

"That's my cue to split, guys. Negotiating really isn't a spectator sport."

After she'd left, Coulter raised a brow. "So you and she . . ."

"Let's get back to the matter at hand," Scott said. Wilders rarely discussed their personal lives with family members, let alone strangers. He mentioned a monetary sum, purposely low-balling it.

Coulter's gaze was mocking. "And here I thought my talents were in demand?"

After a bit more haggling they finally agreed on an amount and shook on it.

"You've got quite a grip there, Wilder," Coulter said. "Must be from squeezing blood out of all those turnips."

Scott grinned. "Must be." His family didn't get rich by paying full price, ever. "So, if you could come by tomorr—"

"Is there a place around here I could crash temporarily?"

"I can get a list of motels for you."

Coulter rubbed his chin. "You could do that. Only I need a place to stay tonight."

Scott knew where this was going. Damn his polite upbringing. "You're welcome to stay here. For a night or two," he added.

Coulter's lips curved in a slow grin. "Well, that's mighty nice of you . . . roomie."

Scott needed a drink. He poured himself an ounce of single malt, and when Coulter proffered his empty glass, refilled that too.

"Say boss, seeing as how you're an expert on all this ESP and me stuff, tell me why I can suddenly move people with my mind when I couldn't before."

Scott had been thinking about this. "This may sound simplistic and unscientific but you never had the proper motivation. People do things they never thought they could while under severe stress. You had the capability all along. There was just no need to call it forth."

"I wonder what else I can do," Coulter mused.

Scott lifted his glass in a toast. "That's what we're here to find out."

22

Sunglasses shading her eyes from the morning sun, Anjali gazed out the window as they entered Napa Valley. The Golden Gate Bridge was an hour behind them, now hills carpeted with lush vineyards stretched out on either side of the winding road.

Their destination was the Adagietto Inn, and that was pretty much all she knew. Instead of briefing her on the case during the drive up, Scott had let loose a volley of complaints against Coulter.

Anjali had sat quietly, listening to the rant. She knew Scott wasn't a complainer. It took something big for him to lose his cool, and the fact that Coulter was God-knows-where, instead of in the car with them heading to Napa, was big.

"And for someone who can move things with his mind,"

Scott continued. "He has a hard time picking his wet towels off the bathroom floor."

Anjali turned away from the window and smiled. "Sounds like you're winding down."

The corner of his mouth curved up. "I think I finally got it out of my system. Thanks for letting me vent. You want to hear about the case now?"

Her smile widened, and she turned back to gaze out the window at the view. "So, this job came your way because your parents are Garrison and Penelope Wilder of *the* San Francisco Wilders, founding family, supporter of the arts, regular appearances in the society pages, personal friends of the governor?"

Scott shot her an amused glance. "Mother ran into Lance David at a museum showing last weekend—"

"And just happened to mention that her oldest son is a paranormal investigator?"

"I'm not clear on how the subject came up, but Mother can make conversation with anyone on anything. As it turns out, Lance and his partner, Ian—"

"By partner you mean—"

"Business and otherwise. Lance and Ian have owned and operated the inn for about four years now. I've never stayed there but I'm told it's quite the place. Rooms are booked six months in advance. That's why they decided on a new addition."

"Ah . . . the new addition. Ominous music builds."

"A month ago they began digging to put in the new supports and that's when they found the bones."

"Indian burial ground? And by Indian I'm referring not

to myself but to a much taller race of people—Native Americans."

"Close but no. The bones were European, old, about four hundred years—according to the people from Berkeley. Lance and Ian wanted to give the bones a proper burial, but the Berkeley team wanted to take them back for examining. And since the bones were uncovered, strange things have been happening at the inn."

"Like what?"

"Mysterious lights, furniture rearranged or broken, bedcovers flung off. Both men have been locked out of the house, twice while not wearing any clothes. The situation became bad enough that Lance told the Berkeley team to forget the respectful burial, take the bones and be done with it. But they can't."

"Can't? You mean won't. They prefer to study the bones in their burial place?"

"No, I mean can't. They've tried removing the bones several times. The first time a heavy ladder fell on the lead member of the crew, giving him a serious concussion. The second time a swarm of red ants prevented them from getting anywhere near the bones."

"The third time?"

"The third time they said to hell with it and went back to Berkeley. Lance and Ian are currently staying in town. So it's just you and me."

Outside, clouds passed before the sun, plunging the countryside into sudden gloominess. Anjali shivered. "Versus a pile of bones."

*   *   *

The Adagietto Inn overlooked manicured vineyards and the nearby Napa Valley hills. Anjali imagined standing under a garden trellis or sitting on the deck in the morning, watching the sun rise over the mountains.

Surely a complimentary suite was the standard exchange for successful ghost-busting activities?

Before exploring the inside, Scott wanted to check out where construction of the new addition was taking place. They crossed the grounds, heading toward the back of the inn and walking through gardens bursting with color.

The ground was gutted at the site of the construction and partly covered by a tarp. Anjali peered into the pit, but it was hard to see anything.

Scott climbed in to get a closer look. The ground was wet in certain spots, and he nearly lost his footing. Stepping over a limp bag of cement, he crouched down in front of what looked like a pile of brown brittle twigs. "Nothing but a pile of bones," he called out.

He reached out his hand, and Anjali gasped. "Don't touch them!" Scott looked up at her, hand shielding his eyes. She was getting a peculiar feeling. Almost like a buzzing. Her skin felt tingly.

In a matter of minutes, he was back beside her and pulling out a set of keys. "Let's check out the inside."

But the back door was ajar. Scott frowned. "The house is supposed to be locked up tight."

"Do you feel that?" she asked as they walked in.

"What?"

"A vibration, sort of like a humming."

"No." He looked at her curiously. "Sense anything else?"

She shook her head.

Scott peered up at the landing thoughtfully. "I'll take the second floor. Why don't you—"

"There are only nine bedrooms," she said firmly. "We can check them out together."

As they moved slowly up the stairs, Anjali gazed around her. Under normal circumstances, she would have been charmed by the interior of the inn. Old original woodwork antiques mixed in with modern artwork and gorgeous European accessories. Checking out the bedrooms, she ran her hands over the exquisitely soft sheets—at least nine-hundred thread count—and took note of the fireplace and two-person whirlpool tub—one for each room

Her mind continued to catalog the decadent details while the air grew dryer. Her arm brushed against Scott's, and the sparks of static electricity snapped between them.

There was something here all right, but she couldn't isolate what or who it was.

Downstairs a door slammed shut.

Anjali was positive they'd left the back door closed.

The humming intensified and rose to a loud buzzing.

She covered her ears, but it didn't make a difference. The sound pounded and echoed inside her head.

Scott grabbed her arm. She could see his lips moving, but it was as if he were speaking underwater. The words came to her garbled.

The chandelier above her head began to swing. In unison, each one of the bedroom doors opened and then slammed shut.

"Let's go." Scott pulled her down the stairs. He grabbed the handle of the front door but it wouldn't budge. He fiddled with the lock, but this time the door really was being held shut by an unnatural force.

"I saw a pair of French doors," Scott said. Quickly, she followed him into some sort of study. The moment she stepped into the room, the buzzing in her ears stopped.

She took a deep breath. "The noise—"

Her words were cut off as a tremendous force swooped down on her, pressing against her chest. She couldn't breathe.

The pressure intensified. Gasping, she tried to draw breath. Darkness circled the edge of her gaze, and she fell to her knees.

"Anjali!" Scott made a move toward her, and a stack of thick, leather-bound books and heavy metal bookends spilled off the top shelf of the bookcase. He dived to the side, narrowly missing being hit.

On the floor, Scott reached for one of the bookends, raised himself on his elbow, and heaved it toward the glass door, shattering one of the panes. Jumping up, he reached through the opening and turned the handle. Mercifully, the door opened.

He pulled Anjali to her feet, and they raced through the door and into the garden.

Instantly, the pressure vanished and her lungs filled with air.

She took a few deep breaths, Scott stopping to look at her. "Are you okay?"

"Less talking," she gasped. "More running."

They sprinted through the garden and back to the car.

Anjali was panting, her hands on her knees. "What the hell was that?"

Scott leaned against the car hood and brushed his arm

against his damp forehead. "I should have seen it when you mentioned the buzzing and humming. Not to mention the static charge in the air." He shook his head in wonder. "Pure electricity."

She straightened and shot him a look of annoyance. They'd nearly been killed or at least severely injured, and Scott sounded almost dreamy. "Evil electricity. There was a definite personality there. I never met a light bulb that wanted to kill me."

Scott's expression turned serious. "Well, now you have. We've got poltergeists."

23

The ringing of the doorbell startled Coulter out of a deep sleep.

The afternoon sun streamed into the room, and he covered his eyes and groaned.

He'd spent the previous night and most of the morning carousing, and stumbled into Scott's place a little after ten A.M. with a bag full of donuts, a large coffee, and a vague sense he was supposed to be somewhere else.

Right. Working.

Then again, he'd never held an honest job in his life and couldn't expect to get into the swing of things right away. With that justification he'd fallen into the deep sleep of the innocent.

The ringing continued. With a muffled curse, he slid out of bed and into a pair of jeans. He never bothered with pajamas. Why should he when nature had created the perfect skin for him to sleep and stroll around the house in. Much to Wilder's annoyance.

Stumbling down the stairs, Coulter swung open the front door and glared into the face of a kid who looked like the teenage version of Spike Lee. "What in hell do you want?"

The kid gazed back at him with heavy-lidded brown eyes and began to speak in a monotone. "Hello sir, my name is Marcus. I live in a bad area with lots of crime. My mom is a single parent. I'm working hard to keep myself off the street."

Coulter yawned.

Unfazed, Marcus continued in the same dull tone. "That is why I am selling magazine subscriptions. So I can go to sports camp. Because sports keep troubled youths like myself off the street. With just one subscription—"

"Christ, you suck." Coulter leaned back against the doorjamb and crossed his arms. "How you expect to earn a dime is beyond me."

"So you gonna buy anything or what?"

Coulter smirked. "Not on your life."

"Whatever."

"Just out of curiosity, where is this so-called sports camp?" Coulter asked.

Marcus turned to leave. "Hawaii."

Coulter whistled. "Nice. You'll never get there though. You're not hungry enough. The most you're gonna make is a bus ticket back to the projects."

Marcus glared at him.

"I can help you," Coulter offered. "Rich neighborhood

like this filled with liberal white people—you could be flyin' first class to the Islands."

"Why would you want to help me?"

Coulter shrugged. "To get into heaven. Why do you care?"

Marcus stared at him suspiciously.

Coulter couldn't blame him. Why did he want to help the kid? Maybe because he remembered a time when handouts and hustling were the only way he could earn a living.

Hell, that was just last week.

But he also remembered what it was like being Marcus's age and on your own, trying to get a slice of what everybody else had for yourself.

Coulter held the door open. "Might as well come in." Marcus now looked wary. Coulter sighed. "See here, you woke me up from a sound sleep, and the fact that I'm offerin' to help you instead of keelin' over from a bitch of a hangover is a stroke of luck for you. Now I plan on eatin' something and you're welcome to join me." He yawned and stretched. "Come in or leave. Either way, shut the door."

Coulter walked back into the house, scratching his armpit and heading for the kitchen.

After a moment he heard the door shut and the sound of sneaker-clad feet following him.

They ended up ordering a pizza.

Coulter had taken one look in the fridge and turned away with disgust. Marcus had peered in after him. "I've never seen so much organic stuff in my life. What's tofu chocolate?"

Coulter shuddered. "A sin."

Now after five slices and two beers—two Cokes for Marcus (ordered along with the pizza because Wilder didn't have a drop of caffeine in the house)—Coulter sat back and rubbed his stomach. "So what've we learned so far?"

Marcus scratched his head. "The trick isn't to push. The best salesmen in the world are the ones who look casual and make you an offer you can't refuse."

"And?"

"Smile and be charming."

"But?"

"None of that crazy smiling," Marcus added. "And none of that slick charm either. It has to be genuine. So find something about the other person you genuinely like— even if it's something dumb like their breath doesn't stink—and let that show through."

Coulter smiled. "Exactly. You want them to give you their money and then thank you for taking it."

Marcus looked down at a sheet of paper. "About the new pitch, do I have to say I live in the ghetto? I mean, my neighborhood is bad and it's not safe at night or during the day sometimes—"

"You've got maybe a minute to grab someone's attention," Coulter explained. "You want to appeal to their emotions. The word *ghetto* does that. Low-income urban area doesn't have the same grab factor."

Marcus nodded and smiled. "I think I might actually get to Hawaii."

Coulter lifted a bottle of beer. "You'll have a hula girl on each arm before you know it."

"I wish I could see you in action though. You know, like a demonstration."

Coulter grinned. "You think I was gonna toss you outta the nest so soon? There's a diner around the corner that calls itself a bistro. Lots of sidewalk seating. We'll start there."

Marcus frowned. "But what if they don't allow soliciting?"

Coulter shrugged. "We're not solicitin'. We're providin' people with the opportunity to help a fine young man change his life." He pushed his chair back and stood. "Give me a sec to get changed."

"Thanks man, I mean really," Marcus said.

Coulter waved away the thanks and then had a thought. "If you don't sell enough today, come back to the house to-morrow and hit up the dude who lives here. You can't find a bigger bleedin' heart."

Marcus reached for another slice of pizza. "The ghost hunter?"

Coulter raised a brow. "He took me in, didn't he?"

24

By the time they drove back to the city, regrouped, and returned to the inn, it was dark and raining. Scott did a quick check of the upstairs and came back to the lobby wearing a puzzled frown. Everything appeared to be normal.

"Place looks harmless to me," Coulter said.

Scott's gaze moved around the quiet Inn. "Poltergeist activity is usually of a short duration but . . ."

Coulter cocked an eyebrow at Scott. "Poltergeist? As in little blond girl meets bad TV reception?"

"Poltergeist, as in the German word for noisy spirit," Scott corrected. "Do either of you sense anything?"

"The buzzing is gone," Anjali said.

Coulter pressed his hand to his stomach with an exaggerated grimace. "I sense . . . hunger pains."

Scott ignored him. He found the calm unsettling. It reminded him of the quiet before the storm.

"Maybe we scared the spirits off?" Anjali said brightly. "Might as well head back. It's dark and—"

"Coulter, where are you going?" Scott asked.

"To explore the kitchen," he said over his shoulder.

"Are you picking up anything?" Scott felt a tiny thrill of excitement. Was the house reacting to Coulter or vice versa?

"Depends on what they have in the fridge," Coulter replied. "There's got to be something to eat around here." He pushed through the dividing door and left the room.

"We're not leaving, are we?" Anjali said.

Scott reached out and lightly squeezed her shoulder. "This time we know what to expect." He held up the ghost-hunting kit. "We're better prepared."

She frowned. "That's not really comforting. Every time I sit down in a dentist's chair, I know what to expect. Doesn't make it any better."

Scott began unpacking. "We'll set up the cameras in the front room."

"Aren't you worried the poltergeist will damage the equipment?" Anjali asked.

Scott removed his laptop from the case and placed it on the coffee table. "That's what surge protectors and a UPS—uninterruptible power supply—are for."

Anjali cocked her head to the side. "How will that help if the poltergeist smashes the equipment against the wall?"

"It won't." He double-checked that the cameras; audio, light, and UV sensors; and EMF meter were all synched to the laptop.

Anjali pointed to the EMF meter. "Why didn't that pick up anything before?"

"It did," Scott said, "As soon as the doors began slamming and the chandeliers swinging."

"Some early warning system."

He grinned. "You're my early warning system. Between you and this thing . . ." His voice trailed off as the meter began beeping.

Anjali grabbed his arm. "What's going on? Why is it doing that? I don't feel anything!" Her grip tightened painfully, and it was all Scott could do not to wince.

Holding the meter out before him, he began walking forward. Anjali followed, still maintaining her death grip on his arm. The machine's beeping became faster. Scott turned around, moving in a wide circle—difficult to do since Anjali clung to him like a barnacle, making navigation tricky.

They were now at the opposite end of the lobby. "There's something on the other side of this door," Scott said.

Suddenly the door banged open. Anjali screamed and grabbed on to his waist with both arms.

Coulter came through the doorway carrying two bottles of wine.

Anjali let go of Scott and let out a deep breath. "We thought you were a poltergeist."

Coulter set down the two bottles of wine. "The fridge was empty. Luckily I bumped into the wine cellar."

"I'm not sure about this." Scott came forward and examined the bottles. "We're professionals. We shouldn't be delving into their stock."

Coulter shrugged and reached for the bottles. "You're the boss."

"Wait." Scott picked up one of the bottles. "We'll keep the Cab. You can take back the Merlot."

The rain drummed against the roof while Scott paced up and down the lobby.

He'd double-checked the equipment at least a dozen times, asked Anjali and Coulter repeatedly if they "sensed anything," and raided the wine cellar for two bottles of the Pinot.

"What time is it, boss?" Coulter asked, stretching out on a settee.

Scott looked down at his watch. "Three . . . the witching hour.

"More like the infomercial hour," Anjali said. She was sitting on the floor, her back against the wall.

"Do you want a chair?" Scott asked.

She shook her head. "I don't want to be sitting on any furniture in case it starts to move."

A lazy smile drifted across Coulter's face as he looked at her. "Don't worry, Angel, I'll protect you."

Anjali giggled.

A stab of annoyance shot through Scott. He told himself it was due to the frustrating lack of spiritual activity.

Coulter sat up, reached for the bottle of wine on the coffee table, and poured himself another glass. He held out the bottle and looked at them.

"No thanks," Scott said.

Anjali uncurled herself and leaned forward, holding out her empty glass. "You read my mind."

Coulter's lips curved in a teasing smile. "I thought that was your thing, sweetheart."

She giggled again.

Scott rolled his eyes. The man wasn't even that good-looking. Yesterday his mother had dropped by the firm, took one look at Coulter and told him he was the spitting image of a young Paul Newman.

She'd never compared Scott to any actors before. Although she'd once said his eyebrows reminded her of Tyrone Power's.

"What's scarier?" Anjali mused, sitting back down. "An evil alien or an evil ghost?"

"Evil alien," Coulter said. "Ghosts don't usually impregnate drooling babies with acid running through their veins inside you. Right boss?"

"Not that I've heard." Scott walked over to the window and looked out. No spooky faces looked back at him. Nothing but the dark night.

Coulter stretched out his legs and rested them on the coffee table. "Seems to be there's a lot of waitin' around in this business."

Scott stared pointedly at him until, with a sigh, Coulter removed his feet and rested them on the ground.

"Tell me, boss, what is it about all this ghost stuff that gives ya such a hard-on?"

"Since you put it so eloquently," Scott said, "something did happen to me when I was about ten."

"You never told me this," Anjali said. "I've told you all about my childhood."

Coulter snorted. "You chicks and your complicated

childhoods. Y'all assume every guy wants to know your whole history."

Anjali glared at him.

Scott cleared his throat. "When I was ten, Nana Wilder died. Now my grandmother wasn't the warmest of women. She was obsessed with neatness and order."

Coulter snorted. "Apple doesn't fall too far, does it?"

"Yes, I do prefer washing my dirty dishes as opposed to stacking them in the corner of the bedroom," Scott said. "May I continue?"

Anjali smiled. "Please. We want to hear."

Somewhat placated, Scott continued. "Nana didn't like people in the house and she especially didn't like anyone in her bedroom, which was separate from my grandfather's. Everyone was terrified of her."

Coulter tipped the remaining contents of his glass into his mouth. "Makes ya wonder about your grandparents, doesn't it? About what their sex life was like?"

"No it does *not* make me wonder."

"My parents have separate bedrooms," Anjali said. "But that's because my dad snores."

Coulter turned to her. "Snoring ain't too bad."

"But he also coughs from his acid reflux, has trouble breathing from his sleep apnea, and his hair smells like coconut oil. He only has like five hairs but he likes to keep them conditioned."

"Anyway," Scott resumed his story. "After the funeral service, mourners gathered at my grandfather's house. Relatives mingled in dark suits and dresses. Hushed conversations carried on around me. I stood by the window at the bottom of the staircase, watching my older cousins, sleeves rolled up, ties loosened, talking outside. No one paid me any mind. That's when the idea came to me. Slowly, I started up the stairs.

"I kept expecting an adult to pop up behind me and demand to know what I was doing but no one did, and soon I was standing in front of the door to my grandmother's bedroom. For a moment I just stood there, staring at the door. It seemed like a long time before I reached for the doorknob. And then I was in, the door shut behind me."

"What did you see?" Anjali asked, eyes wide.

"Well, I'm getting to that," Scott said.

She looked sheepish. "Sorry. I'm one of those people who reads the ending of a book first."

Scott took another sip of his wine, relishing his role as storyteller. "I gazed around the bedroom. The walls were completely bare—no artwork of any kind. The cream duvet covering the heavy four-poster bed was pulled tight, smooth, not a single wrinkle. I peeked under the bed. Enough space for a person to hide but there was nothing, not a speck of dust.

"The dresser was bare except for a silver tray of glass perfume bottles. Her closet was perfectly organized, hatboxes stacked neatly on the upper shelves, each hanger spaced perfectly apart. The room did have one personal touch—a black and white photograph in an oval frame on the nightstand. Naturally, it was of Nana herself."

Scott could see the photograph in his mind clear as day. His grandmother's dark hair scraped back into a severe bun. Under thick straight brows, her eyes were cold, lips pressed into a thin line. The memory still unnerved him. "I was about to leave the room," he continued, "when I felt a little rebellious. So I rearranged the pillows on her bed. I took the perfume bottles off her dresser and—"

"Not really experienced with rebellion, were you, boss?" Coulter said, amused.

"Obviously not," Scott replied. "But I wasn't going to trash the room. I just wanted to rumple it up a bit. I hid the perfume bottles inside a dresser drawer. I rumpled the bed-cover. And then I took her photograph and placed it face-down. Quietly, I left the room and I was barely at the head of the stairs when guilt hit me. Nana was dead and this was how I paid my respects?

"I quickly retraced my steps, opened the door, and I was halfway across the room when I stopped dead in my tracks. The perfume bottles were back on the tray. The bedcover was pulled tight, pillows neatly arranged. The photograph was upright and facing me. And it was cold inside, much colder than it had been before."

Coulter rubbed his jaw and looked thoughtful. "You're sure one of your little cousins wasn't hiding in the room and put everything back?"

"No, I explored every inch of that room. And I was only gone for a few moments."

Anjali shivered. "Don't tell me you saw her."

"I didn't exactly stick around. I ran downstairs so fast I fell and rolled down half the stairs, but I kept going. I didn't stop until I was outside, the sun warm on my face, and with living, breathing people around me. It was months before I could fall asleep with the lights off. But eventually my fear did turn to interest."

A shrill piercing ring broke through the quiet.

All three of them jumped.

"Shit!" Coulter nearly dropped the glass he was refilling.

"Sorry." Scott pulled out his cell phone but the ringing stopped before he could answer. He checked to see the number of the missed call but the phone went dead. "That's odd . . . I charged the battery this afternoon."

"Scott!" Anjali said sharply. "The buzzing. It's back."

The lights in the room began blinking on and off.

And then all hell broke loose.

25

Looking around the room at the blinking lights and the shaking tables and chairs, Coulter had one thought and one thought only.

Jesus Christ Almighty, I'm gonna be on the cover of People!

Well hell, they should alert the media. Call Oprah! Screw the fat girls crying over their weight.

Anjali was crouched in the corner, hands covering her ears. "Can't you hear it?"

"Huh?" He snapped back to the reality in front of him.

"Coulter, what do you feel?" Scott shouted.

What was he feeling?

A strange charge snapped through the air around him. It traveled along the backs of his arms and down his spine.

The lights in the foyer kept flashing on and off. Coulter felt as if he were in one of those clubs with a strobe light.

He stared at the flashing bulbs, focusing. He could feel the energy swelling inside him, pulsing at the same beat as the flashing lights. He imagined reaching out and grabbing the bulb, holding it in his palm, willing the flickering to slow down and stop.

The flashing stopped. The lights stayed on.

Hot damn!

Then he noticed his breath fogging up. The room had grown cold. The chandelier above his head began swinging. He focused on it, and this time felt a strong counter-energy pull fighting him. The chandelier began to sway and pitch dangerously. He concentrated, reaching out from his center. The swinging stopped.

Anjali's hands dropped to her side, and she slowly stood up. "The buzzing . . . it isn't gone, but it's softer."

"I did that," Coulter said. "Ya'll can thank me."

"Poltergeist meet the Coultergeist," Anjali said.

Scott looked at him, amazed. "Tell me, did it feel like you were absorbing the energy from the poltergeist or deflecting it—"

"I felt like I was holding or restraining it. I think I made it mad. The chandelier was much harder to control."

"Ah, guys?" Anjali stood there, hands on her hips. "What's the plan?"

"Try to make contact now," Scott suggested.

She closed her eyes. "It wants us to leave."

"I gathered that," Scott said. "What else?"

"I don't know. It's hard to isolate any feelings or emotions. It's like this thing isn't human anymore but distorted."

A crackle of electricity suddenly surged, and the floral

arrangement on the front desk exploded in a burst of petals.

Anjali opened her eyes. "I can't get through. How am I supposed to show this thing the light when I can't even communicate with it?"

The paintings on the walls flew off and fell to the floor.

"Forget showing this thing the light," Coulter said. "Shove it through the goddamn opening."

Scott didn't look convinced. "But we need to learn more, study this. If I could observe more of its interactions with—"

"Scott!" Anjali had a pained expression on her face.

"Okay." He rubbed his forehead. "This thing was human once. Let's destroy the bones."

Coulter cracked his knuckles. "Got any lighter fluid?"

"But . . . but . . ." Anjali looked torn. "Shouldn't we have some sort of service or something?"

"We are—a cremation," Scott said. "Fire is a purifying element. Let's go."

Pushing his wet hair off his face, Coulter glared down at his muddy snakeskin boots. Here he was standing in a muddy pit in the rain, pouring lighter fluid over a pile of brittle bones, when just a few miles away people were drinking wine, eating filet mignon, and laughing over how fortunate they were.

Napa Valley my ass, he thought.

Even the sight of Anjali holding a flashlight, wet T-shirt plastered to her body, couldn't arouse his interest . . . much.

"Don't you need to pour salt over the bones or something?" Anjali asked. "They always do that in the movies."

Scott brushed the water from his eyes. "I'm all about the low-sodium diet. Besides, that's an old wives' tale."

Anjali smiled back at him. "Superstition has no place in the paranormal world."

Now they were both smiling at each other.

Coulter rolled his eyes. "Can you two stop flirting so we can get on with this? I've got denim up my ass crack."

Scott pulled out a pocket torch from his bag. "Windproof and rainproof." He looked at Coulter. "All I need is for you to keep the poltergeist at bay while I try to get a fire going." He crouched down in front of the bones with the lighter.

"It's here," Anjali said, just as what felt like electrical pin-pricks began piercing Coulter's skin.

"Look at this," Scott whispered as the bones began an eerie, quivery stirring.

Anjali shivered, the light from the flashlight wavering. "Please hurry."

Coulter concentrated on the electrical force surrounding them and tried to restrain it as before. "I don't know how long I can keep this thing away, boss."

The lighter flared and Scott touched it to the fuel-soaked bones. The fire sputtered lazily to life but held.

Anjali held up her hand. "Listen."

A deep moan rose up from the burning bones and ascended like a gust of wind. The mournful call spread out through the soaked hills and was gone.

Then it was just three people standing in a dark, muddy pit.

I don't get paid enough for this, Coulter thought.

26

"Anjali, it's Zarina. Can you buzz me up?"

Anjali groaned. It was almost seven and Coulter would be over any minute. They were going to see a movie. What the hell was her sister doing there?

"Anjali?"

"Sorry," she said and hit the buzzer.

Kali, who'd been sleeping peacefully on the sofa, raised her head. "Run and hide," Anjali warned. "She's coming."

She opened the door and leaned down to fiddle with her sandal strap. It was a casual get-together, not a date. But Anjali couldn't remember the last time she'd had an attractive—make that beautiful—man over. Not that she liked him only because of his looks. She wasn't that shallow. But a beautiful—make that exquisite—exterior certainly didn't hurt. Besides, what was she supposed to do?

Judge people by their auras? She suspected biology was to blame. She felt a deep, primordial thrill whenever she was around Coulter, as if her ovaries sensed his superior genetic material.

Zarina walked in and perched gingerly on the edge of the sofa, her petite frame barely making a dent in the cushion. She and Kali eyed each other with dislike. "Do you know what pet dander can do to the air you breathe?"

"I like it," Anjali said. "Adds texture."

Zarina gave her the once-over. "You're wearing too much makeup."

"I am?" She walked into her bedroom and studied her appearance in the wall mirror. She'd tried for the natural look. Then again, it took a lot of makeup to achieve the natural look. She squinted and pursed her lips. Nah, she looked good.

She took a seat next to Kali and said in a bright false voice, "What brings you to San Jose?"

"I spoke at an all-day conference in Redwood Creek. By the way—" Zarina pulled out a business card from her suit pocket. "I met a representative from Hunter Pharmaceuticals. Their programming department is hiring." She set the card on the coffee table. "I set up an interview."

Ever since their dinner at the Sunset Grill, Zarina had been calling nearly every day about interviews and potential job offers. Happily, Anjali hadn't been home to take most of the calls and her cell phone was permanently on voice mail. "I appreciate the effort but—"

"What's going on with you?" Zarina asked. "Are you depressed?" She pulled out her BlackBerry. "I have a colleague who can prescribe something. Normally I frown on medication but . . ."

"I'm not depressed. Not now anyway. I'm just figuring things out."

"The whole family is worried about you."

Anjali could feel her irritation growing. Well, two could play that game. "You know . . . I spoke to Mom yesterday. She's not fixated on my single status these days. What she wants is a grandchild. That's your department." She expected a sharp retort from her sister and was surprised at the flush that bloomed in her cheeks.

"Vijay and I have been trying," Zarina mumbled. "Well . . . we were trying, but he's always tired and . . ."

"Umm." Anjali cleared her throat. "If you want to, ah, talk about it . . ."

"There's nothing to talk about," Zarina said tightly. "Not about me. If you don't want a job, fine. I don't know what you're doing with your life, but I'm tired of trying to help. You're on your own."

Anjali could feel her own cheeks getting warm but from anger, not embarrassment. "You're tired of trying to help? Since when is perpetual disapproval helping? Getting that from Mom is one thing. But from my sister? And guess what? I have a job. I'm the resident psychic for a ghost-hunting firm! Well one of two, actually."

Zarina stood. "You've got to be kidding me! Have you told Mom and Dad? You're going to give them each a heart attack!"

"I think they're stronger than that. Besides, if anything I did up until now didn't kill them . . ."

"Why can't you pretend you're like everyone else?" Zarina argued. "What's the big deal about this psychic thing anyway?"

Anjali stood as well. "Pretending I'm someone else hasn't worked so well for me—in case you haven't noticed. And you're the one making a big deal about all this—you, Mom and Dad. I have a job I'm growing to like. Coworkers I definitely like. And I'm making a difference. I don't spend nights crying into my pillow or mornings contemplating pouring vodka into my cereal."

Zarina glared at her. "Mom and Dad moved to this country to give us a better life. So we could be successful. What are you doing?"

"No, they moved here to give us opportunities, and opportunity means having a choice. The choice to live our lives any way we want."

The doorbell rang.

Zarina picked up her purse. "I should go."

Anjali went to the door and opened it. "Hey Angel," Coulter said and strode in, looking like Apollo in tight jeans and a white T-shirt.

"Hey—" Anjali began and heard a thump.

Zarina stood there, purse fallen to the floor, lips parted, absolutely mesmerized.

"Ah . . ." Anjali looked at her sister and then at Coulter, who obviously didn't think there was anything odd about the woman in a near-Zombie trance staring at him. He was probably used to just such a reaction. Anjali could more than understand.

But not from her sister.

Zarina had never been gaga over anything or anyone. She planned her life with the ruthless efficiency of the Chinese government. She'd chosen her husband by charting out his potential wage earnings and life expectancy.

She'd never once cried over a movie or oohed over a puppy.

Anjali came to a conclusion: The more repressed they are, the harder they fall.

Since they couldn't stand around and stare at one another, Anjali decided to make introductions. "Coulter, this is my sister, Zarina."

He smiled lazily. "Well isn't your daddy lucky to have such a fine pair of daughters."

"Thank you," Zarina said shyly.

Kali jumped off the sofa and began rubbing back and forth against Coulter's legs. When he picked her up and began scratching under her chin, she closed her eyes in ecstatic bliss.

Anjali could swear Kali had shot her sister a triumphant glance just before shutting her eyes.

"I was thinkin'," Coulter began and put Kali down. Before he could straighten, she jumped back in his arms.

Zarina frowned. "Your cat has no manners."

Coulter laughed and resumed holding the cat. "As I was sayin', how 'bout a change in plans? Drinks and food instead. You wouldn't believe the birdseed Wilder keeps in the fridge."

Zarina giggled.

Coulter smiled at her. "You'll be joinin' us, right?"

"I'd like that."

"What about Vijay?" Anjali reminded her. *What about the argument we just had?*

Zarina turned a distracted smile to her. "Hmm?"

The three of them ended up taking Anjali's car.

27

"Why'd you turn off Slayer?" Coulter demanded. They were driving along an isolated mountain road; majestic pine trees filled the valley below.

"Because I can't think with all that screaming in my ear," Scott replied from behind the wheel. They'd started the drive to the California/Nevada border three hours ago and should have reached the location. "Okay I'm lost." He stopped the car and they all piled out.

Scott spread the map on the hood of the Range Rover while Anjali and Coulter stretched their legs. "I specifically requested an updated DVD for my GPS. I can't find the damn turnoff anywhere and neither can the navigation system."

An icy wind blew over the tops of the trees. The quiet was complete; not even birds twittered in the trees. Civilization seemed far behind. "Do you sense anything?" Coulter asked Anjali.

She gazed around at the isolated point and shivered. "Yeah, the Donner party and they're hungry."

Scott thumped his finger on the map twice. "We're going the right way. The turnoff to the house should be just ahead."

They all piled back in.

The farmhouse was barely standing.

Ragged weeds covered the ground. The wooden planks covering the porch were rotten in some places, worn everywhere else.

"This is a dump," Coulter said as they drove up.

"The place doesn't matter. Rhett Uglee is still a client," Scott said.

He parked the car, and they headed up the dusty, weedy drive. The front door, barely on its hinges, opened and a thin, anemic-looking man with skinny arms, light brown hair in a mullet cut, sideburns, and a droopy mustache came out. He was wearing a sleeveless flannel shirt and a baseball cap turned backward.

Scott held out his hand with a smile. "Rhett?"

Rhett shook hands and gazed curiously at Anjali and Coulter while lighting up a cigarette. "So you wanna talk out here or inside?"

"How about inside?" Scott said. "Anjali can get a feel of the place."

"Angela?"

"Anjali," she said.

"That's what I said. Angela."

"Why don't we go in?" Scott said, and Rhett led the way.

The inside wasn't much better than the outside. Cracked and splintered floorboards, chipped and peeling wallpaper, and beat-up furniture.

"Uglees have lived in the Manor for generations," Rhett said.

Coulter laughed. "Manor?"

"Fill us in, Rhett," Scott said. "On the phone you said you believed the presence was female?"

They all sat down. The chair Coulter sat on buckled and cracked under him.

Rhett's cigarette smoke swirled around the room, and Anjali sneezed.

Rhett settled back and scratched his stomach. "There's a female ghost in my house, and she's been molesting me."

Scott reached over and switched on the video camera.

"I can't bring none of my lady friends home," he complained. "She don't like that. She gets angry and starts messin' with my TV channels."

Anjali bit down on her lip to keep from laughing.

Coulter had a very skeptical look on his face.

Scott kept his tone professional. "Has the presence threatened you at all?"

Rhett shook his head and took another drag. "No, but sometimes she startles me—I scream when that happens. Doors keep poppin' open all the time and such."

"Why don't we take a look around?" Scott said.

Rhett turned to Anjali. "She won't like you bein' here, Angela. She'll think you're one of my lady friends."

Anjali widened her eyes at Scott, who quickly stood up. "How about that tour?"

Rhett shrugged and took them through the house. In the

bedroom, he pointed to the lumpy twin bed. "Sometimes she crawls in there with me."

Coulter leaned close and whispered in Anjali's ear, "You reckon there's ever been a woman within ten feet of this room?"

Anjali smiled, and Scott looked over at them for a long moment before addressing Rhett. "Where else have you experienced strange phenomena?"

They followed Rhett down to the cellar. Old shelves were filled with rows and rows of glass bottles. Dim lighting illuminated cobwebs and the dusty floor. Rhett pointed to one of the shelves. "Once, I was walkin' here . . . and a head popped out between the bottles and starts starin' at me."

"Holy shit, no wonder you're seeing things!" Coulter was holding one of the bottles and sniffing it. "Moonshine."

He held the bottle out to Scott, who sniffed it and yanked himself back. "Damn that's strong."

"I'm tellin' ya'll she's here," Rhett said. "I've tried to make her leave. I tells her, 'You're deceased and I'm not so you best leave me be.' But she don't listen."

They walked back to the main room. Scott took Rhett aside. "I'm going to talk to my associates. We'll decide how to pursue this case."

"I'll be here." He lit up another cigarette and plopped down on the sofa.

Scott, Anjali, and Coulter met outside.

"There's nothing in there," Coulter said. "Are you going to pursue every claim made by a moonshine-swigging nut job?"

"I didn't pick up anything, Scott," Anjali said. "Maybe he's just hearing things. Those floorboards creaked more than my grandmother's knees."

"Now that we're here, I want to give him the benefit of the doubt," Scott said. "We have to be as thorough as possible. According to the local sheriff, one of his female deputies did sense a threatening presence while investigating a theft on the property."

"Theft?" Coulter said. "What would anybody steal from here?"

"Are ya'll going to communicate with the spirit or what?" Rhett called out from the doorway.

Scott looked at Anjali and Coulter. He nodded to Rhett. "We'll be there."

Rhett hovered near the doorway. "I was thinkin' we should make the spirit jealous so she'd come out. Maybe Angela here and I can sit together and she can pretend to be my lady friend."

"I don't think—" Anjali began.

"Actually," Scott said, "that might be a good idea."

She grabbed him by the hand and pulled him aside. "I'm not cozying up to Rhett."

"All you have to do is sit on the sofa with him and talk."

Anjali frowned. "Fine, but this goes above and beyond the call of a medium."

Scott set up the video camera so it faced the sofa where Rhett and Anjali would be sitting. He attached a miniature broadcasting unit to the camera. "This has a radius of one hundred and fifty yards so we'll be able to hear and see everything that happens." He held up his PDA. "We can watch on this. It has a receiving unit."

"How do you know all this stuff?" Coulter asked.

"The guys at Best Buy helped me out."

28

"So," Anjali said. "Is there a special woman you're try-ing to get to know?"

Rhett shook his head. "There was Patty but she's busy with her great-grandkids now."

"I like your house," she said, unsure of what else to say.

"It's my inheritance. Hey, maybe we should sit closer. Otherwise she might know we're just foolin'."

Anjali grudgingly moved half a cushion closer.

"You're much prettier than Patty," he said.

"Thanks."

"Your hair is so black and shiny, like a Labrador's coat."

Shakespeare, Rhett wasn't. "You like Labradors?" she asked.

He shook his head. "They're mean dogs. Not as mean as golden retrievers though. They're the meanest."

"They look it." Anjali crossed her legs and waited.

After a moment she turned to see Rhett staring at her. She quickly turned away.

"Your lips look real soft too," he murmured.

Oh God. If he told her they were as soft as a Labrador's, she'd gag.

She looked directly into the camera in front of her and glared.

Rhett slid over, closing the gap between them. "What is that sauce your people like to eat? The one with the onions and the tomatoes?"

"My people?"

"It's real hot. I've had it with a taco before."

"Salsa?"

"That's right. Mexico food sure is tasty."

Anjali opened her mouth to correct him about her ethnicity and then closed it. What was the point?

"Golden retrievers sure are mean," Rhett said. "One of 'em could kill ya in a heartbeat."

That's it, Anjali thought. If there was a ghost, she was going to make an appearance now.

Anjali turned toward Rhett and smiled. "Your mustache sure is cute," she said. "And I do love salsa. I find it . . . spicy." She curled up on the sofa next to him and flipped her hair over her shoulder. "I like a strong, well-built man like yourself." She reached out and squeezed one of his bony arms. "No wonder your ghost is jealous."

Rhett stared at her, his eyes drifting down to her lips, and he leaned forward.

She forced herself to sit still as his pale, anemic face moved closer and closer and—

He burst into a horrible hacking smoker's cough.

Anjali leaned over and hit him on the back a few times.

And the room suddenly became cold.

With her hands still on Rhett, she looked around the room. Now she could feel something all right.

Rhett had been telling the truth all along.

The jealous female had arrived.

Anjali looked right at the camera. "It's getting cold in here, guys, but . . ." She paused. "I can handle this."

Rhett yelled up at the ceiling. "Angela's my lady friend, you best leave her alone."

Anjali stood up. She could feel anger and bitterness rushing toward her.

She reached out with her mind. The presence was tied to her own circle of bitterness and anger, and Rhett and his lady friends were just a catalyst.

So Anjali closed her eyes, opened the doorway of light, and eased the spirit through.

The air warmed.

Anjali turned to Rhett and put her hands on her hips. "Well, Rhett, looks like your farmhouse has a vacancy."

"I want to kiss you, Angela."

"There isn't enough moonshine in the world, Rhett."

29

The next morning they were on their way back to the city, having spent the night in Reno. Coulter was driving, Scott sat in the passenger seat, while Anjali lay in the back sleeping.

"I think we should request a limousine for our next case," Coulter said. "Do you think Colin Farrell has to drive to and from the location when he's on a shoot?"

"We're not exactly movie stars," Scott replied.

"Not yet. It's only a matter of time before a movie is made about us, and I'll be damned if I let them cast Owen Wilson to play me. Only I can play me."

Scott stretched. "Well, I suppose Tom Cruise could play me then."

"Tom Cruise?" Coulter raised an eyebrow. "Please. Tony Randall maybe."

"Tony Randall passed away."

"What about that Niles Crane dude?"

Scott opened in mouth to answer. And then he saw the girl. She was standing in the middle of the road. She wore a light blue and white gingham dress, covered with an apron. Her hair was a mass of perfect sausage curls. "Stop!"

Coulter slammed on the brakes, but it wasn't fast enough and they ran right into her.

It was like driving through air.

Scott jumped out of the car with Coulter behind him. The little girl was still standing in the same place.

"Is she a freakin' ghost?" Coulter asked.

"Oh my God," Scott whispered. "It's Nellie Olesen."

"Huh?" Coulter said.

Scott continued to stare straight ahead at the girl. "You know, from *Little House on the Prairie*."

"Did you play with dolls too, Wilder?"

"It was a good show," Scott said just as the girl turned and darted into the thicket of trees to the side of the road.

Scott went after the girl.

"Shit!" Coulter looked back at the sleeping Anjali and took off after Scott.

Scott was standing outside a saggy wooden fence bordering a small property when Coulter caught up to him. "So where is she?" Coulter asked.

"I don't know. I saw her just a moment ago."

"I don't think we should be here," Coulter said, looking around.

A dilapidated cabin stood in the center of the fenced-in border. Small pockets of dead grass and gravel made up the front and back yards. On the hole-infested porch was a scarred wooden rocking chair and a rusty toolbox. "There she is." Scott pointed.

Looking out at him from one of the dusty windows was the blond girl. "Come on," he said and went into the yard. Coulter sighed and followed.

They crossed the yard and went up to the porch. One of Coulter's feet went right through a rotten board. "God-damn it!"

"Quiet," Scott said. He tried the door, and it opened easily.

Coulter stepped aside and gestured for Scott to precede him. "I've got your back."

Scott glanced around the small room. An old stovepipe stood in the corner. A tattered braided rug covered part of the floor. The girl stood at the window, looking at him. Sunlight filtered in through the dusty pane and made her golden hair gleam. She was smiling.

"Ah, Scott?"

"Shh." Scott put a finger to his lips and moved forward.

"Really, man, I think you'll wanna hear this," Coulter insisted.

"We have to find out what she wants. Why don't you go and get Anjali and—" He stopped as cold steel was pressed against the back of his neck.

"This is breaking and entering," a raspy voice growled.

Slowly Scott put his hands in the air. "I can explain. You have a supernatural being currently inhabiting your domicile."

"And you have a rifle cocked up against the back of your head. Still want to argue?"

"No sir," Scott said.

"Turn around."

Scott kept his hands in the air and did just that. A tall, stoop-shouldered man with a thick mane of gray hair glared at him. He had his rifle trained on Scott. Coulter stood in view, his hands at his sides. "Do something," Scott murmured to him.

Coulter smiled. "Why?"

"Didn't you see the *No Trespassing* sign?" the man demanded.

"I'm sorry, sir, my name is Scott Wilder and I head a paranormal investigations firm."

The man cocked his rifle. "You have thirty seconds to go on and get."

"But you have a ghost—"

"She don't bother me," the man rasped. "She leads silly fools like you here all the time. Now get!"

"See ya," Coulter said cheerily and was out the door and across the yard in a matter of moments.

"But—" Scott began.

"You now have ten seconds," the old man said.

Scott turned to see where the girl was grinning at him. She didn't look cute any longer. "Brat," he murmured.

"Five seconds!"

Scott took off in a flash.

They were back in the car driving. A smile continued to play along the edges of Coulter's mouth. Scott sat rigidly in his seat.

From the back came the sound of a yawn and then Anjali's voice. "Are we almost home?"

"Yeah," Coulter said.

She leaned forward, placing one hand on each of the seats. "So have you guys been entertaining yourselves while I slept?"

"Scott's been keeping me pretty entertained," Coulter said.

Anjali looked at Scott, who continued to stare straight ahead, silent.

"Hey, do you know what the first rule of ghost hunting is?" Coulter asked. "Always look for *No Trespassing* signs."

30

Anjali sat on her sofa and stared at the coffee table. One bottle of Pinot Grigio and one cordless phone. The phone was for calling her parents and finally telling them about her new career. The wine was for courage.

She'd already had two glasses but bravery still eluded her.

She blamed the vintage.

She should have gone with a heartier yield.

Then again, what was the drink of choice for calling one's parents and delivering potentially devastating news?

How about half a liquor store?

She poured another glass, took a large gulp, and grabbed the phone. Kali was stretched out on the windowsill, yellow gaze fixed on her. Anjali patted the spot beside her. "Come here, sweetie, I need your support."

Kali jumped down, bypassed the sofa, and went into the kitchen. Anjali wondered if the Pet Psychic had an easier time communicating with her cat.

"Okay, let's do it." She dialed her parents' number, pressed the phone to her ear, gritted her teeth, and ignored the pounding of her heart.

Her mother answered. "Hello?"

"Hey Mom, it's me."

"Zarina, my favorite daughter! How are you?"

Great, two seconds into the conversation and Anjali was already the bearer of bad news.

"No Mom, it's Anjali."

Her mother didn't miss a beat. "Anjali, my favorite youngest daughter! I knew it was you."

"Nice, Mom. What were you doing?"

"Going through these yoga studio brochures. Your father and I are going to start taking classes."

It figured. Her parents hadn't done a single yoga pose growing up in India, and now it took a studio in Tempe, Arizona, to get them to do it. But then, none of her relatives did yoga, and back when she'd experimented with it, Anjali had been the only Indian person in her class.

"Yoga's good but . . . I have to tell you something. I have a new job."

"When are you coming to Tempe? There's so much to do here. Last weekend your father and I went camping. We made dal over the cookstove and roasted naan in the campfire. Tomorrow we're going boating in Tempe Town Lake."

Anjali had been hearing about Tempe nonstop since her parents had moved there. She wondered if the chamber of commerce was paying them to promote the place. "Sounds like fun, Mom, but about my new job—"

"You have a new job?"

Anjali reached for the glass of wine, changed her mind and grabbed the bottle, taking a hefty swig. "I . . . I'm a professional psychic now, at a ghost-hunting agency."

Her mother was silent.

Anjali could feel a cold draft moving in from Tempe.

"Mom?"

"What do you want me to say?"

"I don't know. I just wanted to tell you. Are you mad?"

"What good is there in being mad?"

"Nothing I guess, I just really needed to tell you. I mean, this is who I am. I don't want to pretend anymore."

"So who asked you to?"

Did she hear correctly? Did she need to whip out the family album and point to people? "Well, you and Dad—"

"*Oof*, your father and I thought we were protecting you. We wanted you to feel normal. We didn't want people looking at you differently."

If there was one thing Anjali had learned from ghost hunting, it was this: You can't cling to the past.

She took a deep breath. "I know, Mom. I do. It can't have been easy raising a psychic child."

"It wasn't so bad. At least you and your sister never did the drugs. Not like that Shivani Jain." Her voice dropped to a whisper. "Did you know she was kicked out of Berkeley? She's going to a junior college now and probably still doing—"

"The drugs," Anjali finished. "So you're really okay with this?"

"I am. But how am I going to tell your father? Are you at least making good money? He'll take the news better if he knows you're making good money."

"Umm . . ."

"There's this Indian family in Tempe—the Tandons. They have three sons. The eldest is a lawyer, but the middle son became a hairdresser. The family was deeply ashamed. They told everyone he was in jail for tax fraud. But then this year, that same son opened a second salon in Phoenix. He now makes more money than the lawyer! The parents are pushing the youngest son into hairdressing too."

"But forcing the youngest son is the same as—"

"How much do you charge for being psychic? The Tandon boy charges three hundred dollars for a haircut. Three hundred dollars!"

"Well . . ."

"You should move to Tempe. There are lots of ghosts here. Better than the ones in San Jose."

"It's too hot in Arizona."

"What are you talking about? Your ancestors all hail from one of the hottest climates on Earth. You should be used to the heat."

"No thanks, but I will come and visit. I'm just glad things are okay between us."

"They are. You're my daughter. You're perfect."

Anjali felt cuddled in the warm embrace of maternal approval. "Aw, Mom—"

"Of course it would be nice if you were married. And maybe you could lose a little weight? And don't drink so much—no man wants to be with an alcoholic."

Anjali quickly placed the bottle of wine on the floor and out of sight.

"And maybe you should try and get one of those TV specials like that James Van Praagh," her mother continued. "He was here in Tempe, you know. I don't know what the big deal is about him. He has those beady eyes and he's not half as pretty as you. You would need to wear less makeup though and style your hair differently and not slouch so much and . . ."

Anjali lay back against the cushion and smiled.

31

$\int$ cott drove around the Embarcadero looking for parking. Tourists thronged up and down the historic boulevard.

"Just try not to hit a streetcar," Coulter said.

"Scott, there!" Anjali pointed to a spot opening up in front of the Harbor Court Hotel.

"Nice." Scott moved forward and was nearly sideswiped by a black SUV that came out of nowhere. He hit the brakes just as the SUV slid neatly into their spot.

"Don't let some soccer mama get the best of you," Coulter said. "Parking is all about survival of the fittest."

"Forget it," Scott said. "This is California. I don't want to get killed over a spot." He was about to hit the gas when the occupants of the black SUV exited. "Vivica," Scott said as the tall redhead strode forward, tailed by three men. "What the hell are they doing here?"

Anjali stared out the window. "That's Vivica?"

Coulter whistled. "We've got a little saying in Tennessee . . . she's hot."

There was a short siren burst from behind them. Scott looked in the rearview mirror and saw the police car. He rolled down the window and leaned out.

As they passed Scott's car, Vivica met his gaze and smirked. "You're blocking the lane. He wants you to move." The henchmen smirked as well.

Scott put the car in gear and made another circle of the Embarcadero.

"There on the right." Anjali pointed. "I think this family is leaving."

They sat there for another ten minutes while the parents loaded up a bundle of kids and all their packages. A little boy around five jumped out of the car and began running, a big smile on his face. His father caught him around the middle and the kid shrieked with laughter.

"Remind me never to have kids," Coulter said in a bored voice.

"I'm a kid's worst nightmare," Anjali said. "An adult who reads minds."

The tension among the group assembled in the dining room of the ocean liner, the *Santa Perla*, was thick.

Anjali figured it was almost as thick as the bad weave on Sly Tullins's bulbous head. Sly—the owner of the ship— gazed at them with watery blue eyes. His face had a tight, stiff expression, and the smoothness of his forehead seemed unnatural considering his wrinkled hands.

Botox, thought Anjali with a curl of her lip. The expensive suit Sly wore served to make him look slick instead of distinguished. And then there was the little fact that he had called up Vivica Bates after hiring them.

"Mr. Tullins," Scott said coolly. "Would you please explain why you hired both my team and Dr. Bates's?"

Sly gave a fake laugh. "Come on . . . two are better than one. What happened to the spirit of competition." He pulled out a handkerchief and mopped his brow.

"You'll have to decide which of us to hire, now," Scott said.

"Surely, Wilder, this ship is big enough for the both of us," Vivica said with a creamy smile.

Coulter leaned forward in his chair. "What's the big deal? Why don't we go head to head with these fellas? Prove we're better than them?"

"Going head to head with Vivica is more trouble than it's worth," Scott said.

Coulter shook his head. "You afraid of a little trouble? Shame on you."

Vivica sidled up to Sly and laid a hand on his arm. "As I told you on the phone, perhaps it would be best if you leave this case to an actual parapsychologist and not a bunch of"—her voice dropped a notch—"amateurs."

Anjali watched the conflicted emotions play over Scott's face. She didn't know the whole history between Scott and Vivica and she wasn't going to do a little peek-and-dash into Scott's mind just to find out. That would be rude. She wasn't some mental Peeping Tom.

Scott looked at them and sighed. He turned around. "You've got a deal, Mr. Tullins. Now tell us about your ship."

Sly waited until they were all seated before beginning his story. "As some of you may know, the USS *Santa Perla* was a troopship during World War II. In November of 1942, while performing routine maneuvers off the Irish coast, the *Santa Perla* sliced through a British cruiser. Almost four hundred British sailors drowned."

"Jesus," Coulter murmured. "Talk about friendly fire."

Sly coughed. "Yes . . . well . . . after the war, the USS part of her name was dropped and the *Santa Perla* was converted into a luxury liner by my great-grandfather. On the inaugural voyage, a starlet, Mary Chestnut, found her beau in the arms of another woman. Mary was later found dead in the bathtub. She'd shot herself in the head."

"I would have shot the beau," Vivica said. "More than once."

Sly glanced at her nervously and continued. "A few weeks after Mary Chestnut's death, a fire in the boiler room caused the death of two engineers."

"On the phone you mentioned the boiler room needs to be looked at," Scott said. "But the electricians you've hired—"

"Can't get near it." Sly said. "As soon as one of the men reaches the bottom of the staircase he's overwhelmed by a choking sensation and can't go any farther. There are power surges, our computers constantly malfunction, and the bathroom of our most expensive suite is constantly overflowing with water."

"Did you call a plumber?" Coulter asked.

Sly wasn't amused. "To answer your question, Mr. Marshall, the top floor suites have been without water for fifty-odd years, the pipes have all rusted away."

Coulter shivered. "Ooh. Spooky."

Sly frowned and looked at Vivica, then Scott. "So what's the plan? I need this ship fixed."

"We'll reconvene tonight," Vivica said. "After I connect with one of my associates."

Sly tugged on his tie. "I—I never said I'd stay on this ship at night."

"Why, Mr. Tullins." Anjali smiled sweetly. "Don't you want to take part in our healthy competition?"

"I suppose . . ."

"Of course Sly will be there," Vivica said smoothly. "He'll see firsthand which team is capable of doing the job."

Coulter winked at Vivica. "Until tonight . . ."

Vivica's mouth tightened and she swept out of the room, trailed by her two men.

"Well, this should be interesting," Anjali said. She turned to the guys. "Venckman, Egon, let's go."

"I suppose I'm Egon," Scott said and followed them out.

32

Vivica glared at the three men. "What do you mean he's gone?"

"His room's empty. All his belongings are still there but he's gone," Gaspar said.

"Find him," Vivica said. "Hurry!" The three men filed out.

Vivica picked up her coffee mug and threw it against the wall. Ceramic shards flew in the air as brown liquid seeped slowly down the wall. "Damn!"

Hans was missing. She had arranged for him to stay in one of the campus apartments. He showed up quietly at the lab every morning at eight for testing and left just as quietly at five. Considering the man had been living off scraps when she found him, the university apartment must have been a veritable oasis.

Why had he left?

*   *   *

Three hours later Hans was discovered at a local school carnival, curled up in the haunted house.

When Gaspar, Maddox, and Fitch came to claim him, they found Hans surrounded by firefighters. "He could have been killed," one of the firemen said. "Someone set fire to several of the rides. Thank God none of the kids were here yet. We haven't found out how the fires started though, no matches, nothing combustible to be found."

Maddox cleared his throat. "Thank you, we'll handle this." He led Hans away; the two other men brought up the rear.

"We have to tell Vivica about the fires," Gaspar said.

Hans walked straight ahead, gray eyes unblinking, a blanket wrapped around his shoulders.

Immediately upon reaching the apartment, Hans fell into a deep sleep. It was obvious he wouldn't be waking soon.

Vivica stared down at her protégé, her face angry. "Damn, damn, damn!"

"What do you want us to do?" Maddox asked.

"You stay here and watch Hans. Fitch and Gaspar will come with me. We'll have to call Odina," Vivica said, annoyed.

"Not her," Fitch groaned.

"Definitely not her," Gaspar chimed in.

Vivica turned on them. "What do you recommend? Do either of you have any psychic power I don't know about?"

The two men stared down at their shoes.

"We have to hire Odina." Vivica's hands curled into fists. "Damn I hate mediums!" She stalked out of the room.

Gaspar glared at Maddox, who was smiling. "You lucky bastard."

33

Promptly at eight o'clock, Scott, Anjali, and Coulter were in the dining room of the *Santa Perla*, waiting.

"I see dumb people," Coulter said, staring out the window.

A few moments later Sly Tullins entered, followed by Vivica, two of her men, and a heavy-set middle-aged woman dressed in a flowing purple robe, with a beehive of yellow hair and at least three layers of makeup. Numerous rings winked and sparkled on her hands.

"So how are we going to do this?" Scott asked.

Sly was looking increasingly nervous as he gazed around the room. "I, ah, think I'll flip a coin. The side that wins calls the shots."

"Well isn't this professional," Scott mumbled.

"What's the matter, Wilder?" Vivica sneered. "Afraid

we'll go first and win or you'll go first and make a complete ass of yourself?"

"I think he's more afraid you'll sink your fangs into him and make him one of your undead," Coulter said. Gaspar and Fitch glared at him.

Vivica turned to the heavy blond woman. "Odina, what do you think of the setting?"

Coulter snorted. "Odina?"

"We shall proceed," Odina thundered. Sly jumped. "The spirits are restless."

"Right." Sly dug into his pocket, pulled out a coin, and flipped it in the air. "Call it!"

"Heads," Vivica said quickly.

Scott shrugged. "Fine."

Sly caught the quarter and slapped it on his palm. "Heads."

"Excellent." Vivica shot Scott a triumphant look.

"We will set up in the southeast corner of the room," Odina ordered. "It is particularly conducive to contacting the spirits."

Coulter rubbed his stomach. "I'm starving. Who do I have to contact to get some food?"

The lights were turned off, candles were lit. A platter of Fisherman's Wharf sourdough bread had been placed in the center of the table. All eight of them sat around the table that had been stripped of the tablecloth and prepared for the séance. "Join hands," Odina commanded.

Anjali took hold of Scott and Coulter's hands. Coulter sat next to Sly and grimaced when they joined hands. "Do you have to sweat so much?" he demanded.

Sly was next to Fitch, who didn't look too happy about sitting next to Odina. On the other side of Odina were Vivica, then Gaspar, and then Scott.

"Now everyone place their left foot on top of the foot of the person to their left," Odina instructed. "Together we form a circle of positivity. No negative energy will be allowed to enter this circle. Those participators who are negative may leave the circle now."

Coulter pushed back his chair. Scott shot him a look. Reluctantly, Coulter scooted back in.

Odina watched them, her mouth a grim, straight line. "Let us begin," she bellowed. "Dearest spirits, we bring you gifts of light, gifts of nourishment, into death. Commune with us, feel free to walk among us."

"Everyone watch your valuables," Coulter said.

"Wilder, either you control your team or leave the room," Vivica said sharply.

Scott gazed pointedly at Coulter. "We'll be quiet."

Odina closed her eyes. "Kind spirits, do not be afraid, we are here to help. Commune with us. Show yourselves. Spirits, we seek to communicate with you from life into death. Why do you haunt this dwelling? We are here to help."

A soft wind blew through the room; the candles fluttered. Anjali squeezed Scott and Coulter's hands hard. Both men looked at her. In the dim light her golden complexion was covered with a thin sheen of perspiration.

Odina raised her voice. "Spirits, knock if you are here. Let the wood of this table be your conduit."

Anjali sat up straight, holding on to the two next to her in a death grip.

"Gentle spirits," Odina said. "You may enter. Let the wood of—"

A loud knock echoed through the room.

"Spirits, are you with us?" Odina's eyes remained closed.

Two knocks in quick succession followed.

Odina opened her eyes. "I am going to allow the spirit to speak through me. The circle must remain unbroken."

A moment passed.

Slowly the table moved in a clockwise direction.

Odina sat still in her chair. "The circle must remain . . ."

Her voice trailed off as a high, tinny voice rose into the air.

The spirit was speaking.

But the voice did not come from Odina.

It came from Anjali.

34

Seven pairs of eyes were focused on Anjali.

"What is it you wish of me?" the voice asked.

Odina's eyes flew open. "No one told me she was a medium," she hissed.

"Wait your turn, Wilder," Vivica snapped.

"She wasn't opening herself up," Scott said. "I don't know what's going on."

Anjali's body was taut. The muscles in her neck stood out. "The host is unwilling," the voice said.

Coulter leaned over and looked at Scott. "Shit, what do we do?"

"Keep holding hands. Don't break the circle," Scott whispered. "We have to wait until she fights it or the spirit leaves."

Anjali's face creased in a smile that was crafty and cunning, wholly foreign to her. "Will you not ask a question?"

"What do you want?" Sly asked.

"My name is Mary and I want this body," the voice said.

"Mary Chestnut was the actress who killed herself in the bathroom of her suite," Sly said excitedly.

"Well, duh," Coulter replied.

"Two mediums may not be present during a séance," Odina insisted, looking sulky.

Suddenly a tremor passed through Anjali's body, and she fell back against the seat.

Scott reached out and checked the pulse on the side of her neck. He touched her cheek. "Anjali?"

Her eyes fluttered open. She shuddered. "The presence slipped in."

"Was it Mary Chestnut?" Sly asked.

"It was definitely a she. Her thoughts were in my head. All I could feel was this violent hate. I think she killed Mary."

Sly shook his head. "Mary committed suicide. Besides, the spirit said she was Mary."

"Spirits do lie," Scott pointed out.

Slowly Vivica clapped her hands. "Well, that was an Oscar-winning performance. Wilder, you've trained her well."

"You saw her face," Coulter argued. "I'm surprised her head didn't start spinnin' around."

"She was definitely possessed," Sly agreed.

Vivica smiled at Sly. "Excuse me, but what you know about mediums wouldn't fit inside of a bumblebee's ass. Possession is very easily faked. I can vouch for Odina; she's

done a number of séances. What you've just seen here is
nothing more than trickery."

In the distance a door slammed, stalling further conversation. The sound of footsteps moved toward them.

Anjali turned to Coulter. "Do you feel that?" she asked.

"Yeah," he said. "A freakish energy or something."

A moment later, one of Vivica's minions walked into the
room with a man Scott recognized. He couldn't forget those
cold gray eyes.

Hans Morden.

Vivica moved quickly toward them. She and her minion
whispered for a few minutes before she turned around.
"Odina, I no longer need your services."

Anjali grabbed Scott's arm. "He's telepathic, isn't he?
That man? He's like me."

Odina remained seated. "I still get paid, right?"

Vivica nodded at one of her men, who pulled out a check
and tossed it in front of Odina.

"But what about my ride?" Odina demanded.

"Get a taxi, you old cow," Vivica snapped. She swept out
of the room with Hans, followed by her team.

"So what's the plan?" Anjali asked. "No way am I doing
another séance."

Scott spread out a map of the ship on the table. "So we
can assume there are two main areas of psychic activity,"
Scott said. "The boiler room and the cabin where Mary
Chestnut killed herself."

"You know, I didn't think this through," Coulter said.
"What are we going to do? Try to run faster than Vivica's
team and clean out these places before she does?"

"Well, they can't be in two places," Scott pointed out. "If

they're in the boiler room, then we'll head for Mary's cabin."

"Where is Mary's cabin?" Anjali asked.

Scott pointed to a spot on the map. "Upper deck, left wing."

Anjali glanced up and cocked her head to the left. "They're in the cabin." Both men turned to face her. "I can feel him, Hans. Can't you, Coulter?"

"Before, not now."

Scott watched her, his expression concerned. "Is Hans communicating with you?"

"Not exactly but you know how sometimes you can be really aware of someone? Their very presence can change the energy of a room."

"I don't like this," Scott said. "Hans is unstable. If he starts pushing into your mind . . . we'll let Vivica have this case."

Anjali felt like a baby. Ooh, the creepy psychic is scaring me. "Forget it," she said. "I can sense him; he can sense me. At least I know where he is and I can avoid him. Let's take a look at the boiler room."

She got up, heading for the door, and then stopped. "Umm, where is the boiler room exactly?"

The boiler room was a case of residual haunting.

The spirits of the dead engineers were trapped in the room, reliving their last moments of running up the steps trying to escape.

Anjali went down into the room, stopping on the last step. She could feel the pressure on her chest, the inability to breathe, everything the two men had faced.

She closed her eyes and cleansed the room in a matter of moments.

Coulter was waiting for her at the top. He smiled. "Done?"

"Done. Where's Scott?"

He shrugged. "Mumbled something about finding Sly. Come on, I want to show you something." He pointed to a light fixture. "Watch this." He stared at the bulb. For a second it flickered and then began to grow brighter and brighter until Anjali had to shield her eyes.

"Forget solar power," she said. "We've got a new energy source."

He grinned. "And I'm one hundred percent environmentally friendly."

The bulb suddenly exploded, and she jumped. Coulter caught her around the middle and swung her toward him, laughing.

He put her down so her back was against the wall and planted a hand on either side of her, blocking her in.

Well, this was unexpected, she thought.

His hand drifted to her hair, and he lazily curled a lock around his finger. "I think you're exotic."

She was finding it hard to breathe. Nothing to do with ghosts. Just hormones. She laughed nervously. "Exotic? Not really. The country is crawling with Indians. We're pretty mainstream."

Coulter's warm breath tickled her ear and his lips grazed the side of her cheek. "Is that right?"

Becoming a professional psychic had certainly done wonders for her love life.

Still.

Beautiful as he was, she wasn't sure about the timing. Not with crazy Hans lurking in her mind. Not when she'd been so recently possessed by a murderous ghost. Not when . . .

His mouth moved over hers. A moment later his tongue parted her lips.

Hai Ram.

Someone cleared his throat.

She felt Coulter pull away and opened her eyes. Looking over his shoulder, she saw Scott standing there.

His face was perfectly smooth, composed. "Hans has disappeared."

"What!" She stepped away from Coulter and reached out with her mind. Nothing. Great, now Hans had gone from lurking in her mind to possibly lurking behind the next corner.

"We'll continue with the investigation. Unless Hans bothers us, he's Vivica's problem," Scott said. "I'm heading to the upper deck. Meet me there." He walked off.

Coulter pulled out a cigarette pack and tapped the bottom. "I've been dyin' for one of these."

Anjali pushed her hair back from her face and straightened her shirt. "That was a little awkward."

"How so?" He stuck the cigarette in his mouth and began searching through his pockets. "Got a light?"

"No, sorry. Well, awkward because . . . umm . . . Scott saw us. We're supposed to be working here."

"Who cares? I thought you meant awkward because Wilder's jealous." He yanked the cigarette out of his mouth and stared at it. "I wonder if I can light this thing myself."

"Scott can't be jealous."

Coulter quirked a brow. "Didn't you see his face? Looked like he'd been punched in the gut."

"It did?" Anjali hadn't noticed. She suddenly felt very clueless for a psychic.

Coulter leaned forward and kissed her on the cheek. "Aren't you cute? Tell the boss I'll meet ya'll in the dead chick's room."

Anjali watched him walk away.

She stood there for a moment until the uneasiness hit. Hans was on the loose and she was all alone.

Which way was the upper deck again? Instead of a sixth sense, why couldn't she have been born with a directional sense?

She'd barely taken a step when Scott's voice crashed into her skull, startling her with its strength.

Anjali!

His voice boomed in her head, and the urgency made her run.

She ran down the metal gangplank, trying to zero in on his presence. She started toward a metal door, then backed up and headed down another hallway.

She reached out, focusing. *Where are you?*

She was in an isolated strip of corridor. On one side was the wall and on the other the railing, beyond that were the bowels of the ship. In front of her was another metal door, and she tried it. Locked.

Anjali.

Scott was here, she could feel him. With a smile of relief she turned around.

But it wasn't Scott who stood behind her.

It was Hans Morden.

35

$\int$ he felt a wave of cold fright slide over her body.

Scott's voice coming out of Hans's head was so wrong.

She backed away from him and moved toward the door she'd just come through.

It slammed shut in her face.

She turned around. Hans's vacant expression was now twisted into something angry. "You can't help Mary."

Maybe if she learned more about the spirit controlling Hans she could somehow force it out? "Who are you?"

"I'm Mary."

Great. They had a schizophrenic spirit on their hands. At any rate, Anjali no longer cared who'd killed Mary Chestnut. She just wanted to get off the damn ghost ship.

Hans moved toward her. "Mary is trapped here. You can't help her."

"I don't want to," Anjali said.

Hans sneered. "I don't believe you."

"Then we have a problem."

Okay, she had to figure a way out of here. She didn't know whether Hans was a willing host, but during the séance, she'd been able to push the presence out of her mind after hearing Scott's voice calling to her, feeling him holding her hand.

"Hans? Hans, listen to me." She kept her voice low and softly reached out with her mind, trying to connect with that part of him not controlled by the spirit. "Hans—"

The thing shoved her, hard.

The moment his hands touched her, it was like a flash-bulb went off in her brain. A woman's face—cupid's bow mouth, dark blue eyes, and chestnut curls, staring at her-self in the mirror, then lunging at the glass with a vicious snarl. The same woman, putting the barrel of a gun in her mouth, hands steady on the trigger.

Anjali lost her balance. She fell back hard, her head making painful contact with the metal. The world shifted out of focus. Hans—Mary, it was Mary—loomed above her, reaching for her. Gray eyes shifting into blue.

No more nightmare-free nights for me, Anjali thought.

If she survived, that was.

She raised her hands to ward off the attack, but then someone was yanking Hans away.

The world shifted back in and she saw Scott push Hans away. The man lost his balance and fell against the railing. He sat there, blinking, and then with a cry, scrambled off, fleeing through the door.

Scott was beside her, brushing the hair from her face. "Are you okay?"

"My head hurts."

His fingers lightly probed the back of her head. "You'll have a nasty bump but the skin isn't broken. Do you feel nauseous or dizzy?"

"No."

He helped her to her feet. For a second her legs felt like jelly, and she grabbed on to his waist to steady herself.

That's when he pulled her into his arms.

She pressed her face against his chest. He felt so solid. "Mary Chestnut committed suicide—out of hate. That's what I kept sensing, self-hate."

Scott pulled away and looked down at her. "How do you feel?"

Like she wanted him to hold her again. "Okay, but Mary is still floating around this ship."

"Vivica can deal with it. Let's get out of here." He started walking and held out his hand behind him.

Smiling, she caught up with him, put her hand in his, and they went to find Coulter.

36

"**W**hat in God's name are you making?" Scott stared in horror at Coulter's creation.

He had crammed ham, pastrami, tomatoes, pickles, jalapeños, cheddar cheese, onions, mustard, mayo, and several juicy slices of mango between two slabs of sourdough bread.

"Remember that mango chutney Angel's sister brought over? I realized that mango tastes good on everything. Makes it tangy." He took an enormous bite, managing not to spill a single drop. "Want some?"

"Not on your life." Scott didn't know what was going on between Coulter and Anjali's sister. The guy made out with one sister and was being fed by the other.

Scott was staying out of it.

When the doorbell rang, he very thankfully left the

kitchen, crossed the hall into the foyer, and opened the door.

Eddie Mirza stood there, a big grin on his face. "You're about to owe me big time."

"Spill it," Scott said.

The three men were seated in the kitchen. Coulter was on his second sandwich, having fixed an identical one for Eddie.

"Well," Eddie began and took a bite. "Hey, this is delicious!"

"I like a man with a sophisticated palate," Coulter said.

Eddie grinned. "Well, you know Vivica and I have never seen eye to eye. So when this project came across my desk I didn't pass it on to her even if she is my colleague."

"Pass on what?" Scott asked.

"The thing is, I'm already committed to a case in Killarney—numerous sightings of free-floating orbs at Dunluce Castle. I've never been to the Emerald Isle. Have you?"

"What's the damn project?" Scott demanded.

Eddie's grin widened. "I'll give you a hint. Pacific Grove."

"The Booth House," Scott said in a stunned voice.

Coulter popped the last bite in his mouth. "What the hell's the Booth House?"

"Supposedly one of the most haunted historical homes in America," Eddie answered.

"Haunted historical home?" Coulter said. "Say that three times fast."

Eddie did.

Coulter shrugged. "Guess it's not that tricky."

Scott cleared his throat. "Back to the Booth House. We

use the term *supposedly* because no one in our field has ever been allowed inside to investigate."

"It gets even better," Eddie said. "Dr. Madison from the NASPR will be on hand as a consultant."

"The NASPR?" Coulter asked.

"The North American Society for Psychical Research," Scott clarified. "Virginia Madison is one of the few parapsychologists respected by other branches of academia." He smiled at Eddie. "Present company included. Dr. Madison has a Ph.D. in American history as well."

"Well la-di-da." Coulter got up and went to the fridge.

Eddie rubbed his hands. "This is gonna really knock your socks off, Scott. Now, if my Dunluce Castle contact wasn't such a pretty Irish lass I'd—"

Scott groaned. "Honestly, Eddie, you take more commercial breaks than must-see TV. Get on with it!"

"Well, it's funny you should mention TV because . . . the Sci Fi Channel will be filming the entire Booth House project! They're sending in a camera crew."

Coulter shut the refrigerator door and slowly turned around. "Did you say the Sci Fi Channel? We're going to be on TV?"

Eddie glanced at Coulter. "You're not camera shy, are you?"

"Is the pope Mormon?" Scott said dryly.

Wearing a big smile, Coulter sat back down. "Well la-di-da, boys."

37

Pacific Grove was a ritzy beach town in Monterey County. Benzes, BMWs, and Ferraris roamed the tree-lined streets like sleek, expensive stallions.

Coulter stood outside the Lighthouse—a popular restaurant overlooking the ocean. He cupped his hand around his cigarette, struggling to light it before the sea breeze blew out the flame. Mission finally accomplished, he took a long drag and leaned back, one foot propped up against the wall. *I could spend the rest of my days in a place like this,* he thought, staring out at the expanse of blue sky and water.

A blond woman in a sweater set exited the restaurant, three adorable blond children in tow. She stared at Coulter with a look of dismay. "Okay kids," she announced. "What do we do when we see a smoker? One, two, three, inhale!"

All four of them held their breaths and ran to their car, a dark blue BMW X5.

Unperturbed, Coulter continued to stand outside and smoke. Several more diners glared at him as they entered the restaurant. He was tempted to light up again, but Scott and Anjali were waiting inside with their guest.

He took one last drag, then flicked the stub to the sidewalk, crushing it under his boot. Maybe Vegas was better suited to his tastes.

Dr. Virginia Madison was a short, stocky woman in her early sixties with enormous blue eyes that peered out at the world from behind rose-tinted glasses. Her thick brown hair was cut in a bob with bangs.

Coulter had the feeling Dr. Madison had worn the same haircut since the fifth grade.

"I'm thrilled the Booth family contacted us and not the ASPR," Dr. Madison said, and beamed at them over a glass of sherry.

Coulter assumed it was sherry.

It looked like donkey piss.

"The ASPR?" Anjali asked.

"The American Society for Psychical Research," Scott explained.

Dr. Madison smiled. "Yes. Not to be confused with my group, the NASPR. The ASPR is based out of Boston. We're based out of San Francisco. And then of course there's the SPR, Society for Psychical Research, which is based in London."

Coulter yawned.

"Are you tired?" Dr. Madison asked with concern.

"No, just bore—"

"He doesn't sleep well," Scott interjected. "Night terrors."

Coulter narrowed his eyes.

"Oh dear," Dr. Madison said. "But then surely this job isn't—"

"Could you tell us more about the Booth House," Anjali asked. "Scott filled us in on most of it but . . ."

"You are the authority," Scott said.

"Oh goody!" Dr. Madison practically bounced in her chair. "I love telling this story. I'll just start from the beginning, shall I?"

Coulter had already heard the story in detail on the drive down and shot Scott and Anjali a pained look.

He was ignored.

"The Booths' Victorian mansion was built in 1880 by Randall Booth for his new bride, Sarah," Dr. Madison began. "Sarah was just seventeen and newly arrived from England. Randall was forty-two. Not uncommon in those days."

"Seventeen?" Coulter mused. "All power to the fella."

"Oh, Booth was quite pleased with the match," Dr. Madison continued. She looked at Coulter. "Oh, not for the reason you think, Mr. Marshall, although I suppose there was *that* too. The marriage was strictly a business match between Booth and Sarah's father. She was bringing quite a dowry with her—the deed to a large estate in Hampshire. Not that Booth needed it. He was worth almost twenty million back then, and in today's dollars—"

"I suppose the man wanted to protect his investment," Coulter said.

Anjali frowned.

"What?" he said. "I'm thinkin' like a man from that time. Isn't that what you're supposed to do as a historian? Walk in their shoes? Not force our modern values on 'em?"

"Er, yes," Dr. Madison agreed.

"Let's continue," Scott said.

"Booth's twin daughters were born soon after the couple moved in. For a while the family was happy; Randall was a known philanderer but he seemed to have settled down."

"Or he was very discreet," Anjali added.

Dr. Madison smiled. "Most likely. But the discretion did not continue. The year the twins turned six, Randall took up with one of the servants. Her name was Molly and she was sixteen."

Coulter ordered another whiskey, neat.

"I think I'll have one of those," Dr. Madison said, looking at his glass. "I don't know why I drink sherry."

"I don't know why you do either," Coulter said and held up two fingers to the waitress.

"Now unlike his other mistresses," Dr. Madison continued, "Molly believed Randall would leave his wife and children and marry her. Imagine her surprise when she discovered Randall in the arms of—"

"His wife?" the waitress asked.

They all looked up. The waitress set down their drinks. "Well . . . was it his wife? I've heard the Booth place is haunted. Everyone here has."

Dr. Madison took a sip of whiskey and smacked her lips. "Delicious! No dear, it wasn't his wife. Wouldn't that have been a twist? Molly found Randall in the arms of a neighbor—a pretty young widow."

"And here I thought history was boring," Coulter said and widened his eyes as Dr. Madison knocked back her drink.

She smiled at the waitress and held out her empty glass. "Would you mind, dear?"

The waitress grinned. "Not at all. This one's on the house if you tell me how it ends."

Dr. Madison clapped her hands. "Oh goody! A fresh pair of ears."

Coulter rolled his eyes.

By the time Dr. Madison resumed the story her cheeks were tinged pink. "Now this is where the account gets a little muddled. On the day of the twins' birthday, Molly put a small amount of poison into the birthday cake. According to one servant, Molly wanted revenge. According to another eyewitness, Molly's intention was to make the girls ill so she could nurse them back to health and maybe win back Randall's favor. Both the twins had two slices of cake each, Randall and Sarah did not have any. By the next day the twin girls were dead. And Molly hanged herself in her room."

"And the bastard Randall was left standing," Anjali fumed. "He was indirectly responsible."

"Wait, I haven't finished," Dr. Madison replied. "One year later Randall was murdered in his sleep. The case was never solved. Sarah passed away in 1922 at the age of fifty-nine. Just before her death she'd contacted a medium to help her communicate with the ghosts of her daughters and husband. It was a closed session, and the next morning Sarah Booth was found dead in her bed. No foul play or suicide, she'd suffered a stroke during the night."

"Five possible ghosts," Scott murmured.

Dr. Madison bounced in her chair. "Isn't that exciting?"

38

They drove up the mansion's gravelly drive, dead leaves and small branches crunching under the tires, and parked behind a dark gray van.

The granite three-story Victorian, graced with gables, balconies, turrets, and every other gothic cliché one could think of, loomed before them. Technically, Scott could find no fault with the architecture of the house, but the more he stared at it, the more unsettled he felt. Perhaps he was just projecting, perhaps he had an overactive imagination, but then he was a paranormal investigator; those traits came with the territory.

Dr. Madison literally bounced out and ran to meet the camera crew. Scott, Anjali, and Coulter followed at a more leisurely place.

Coulter surveyed Dr. Madison as she stepped from foot

to foot, waving her hands, talking excitedly. "The poster child for ADD," he said.

"I like her," Anjali said.

Scott watched her walk away from the house and stare out at the ocean. A cold wind swept from the water and tousled her hair.

He came to stand beside her. "What is it?"

"I don't know. But something is definitely here."

"Come along!" Dr. Madison clapped her hands. "I can't wait to get started."

Jane, Darryl, and Steve made up the camera crew hired to film the Booth House weekend.

Jane, the camera operator, was slender, with short hair and delicate features. She gazed up at the dark mansion and lit a cigarette. "I'd take a brownstone in Brooklyn any day."

"The first thing we should do is set up a base," Scott said.

Dr. Madison led them inside. "Let me show you the sitting room."

They stepped into a hall of dark wood and paneled walls. They followed the professor across a polished parquet floor and into a beautiful room ornamented with brass wall sconces and a crystal chandelier, and dominated by a marble fireplace. A loveseat rested on one end of the room, a full-sized sofa on the other. Diamond leaded glass windows provided the softest hint of light.

"This should do," Scott said and looked at Jane for confirmation. She nodded, and both crews began unpacking the equipment.

Anjali cleared her throat. "I think we should also make

it a rule not to smoke inside. I have sinus problems, and besides, the smell will get into the carpet."

Scott didn't know she had sinus problems.

Jane straightened. She was the only one smoking. "Give me a break."

He could see Anjali getting ready to argue and interrupted. "Anjali has a point. Cigarette smoke can look like psychic manifestation on film. If you want to smoke, please do it outside."

Jane brushed by him on her way out the door. Instead of looking offended, she smiled at him.

Dr. Madison clapped her hands again and beamed at everyone in the room. "Are we ready for the tour?"

They started on the third floor, which once housed the Booth children's bedrooms and nursery. Scott looked at Anjali. "Anything?"

"Nothing specific."

After that they all filed downstairs and through to the back. They stepped out onto a rolling green lawn. The grass sloped down to the sea cliff and an old rusted carousel.

"The carousel," Anjali said. "Something's there."

"I feel it too," Coulter said. "Energy."

"Really?" Dr. Madison reached out with her hand, then pulled it back with a wistful smile. "Come, I've saved the best for last. Ladies and gentlemen, follow me into the dining room."

They stood outside the closed double doors of the dining room like expectant children on a field trip. Dr. Madison paused for effect, Jane switched on the camera, and they entered.

The first thing Scott felt was cold.

"This is it," Dr. Madison said. "This is where the twins' birthday cake was served." Jane circled the room, filming from every angle.

Anjali laid a hand on the dining table. "Don't quote me on this, but I think the twins' poisoning was an accident."

Dr. Madison looked very pleased. "Really!"

They went back to the sitting room, where Darryl and Steve had finished setting up the equipment. "Well," Dr. Madison said. "I can't tell you what a wonderful feeling I have about this project. I'm so gl—"

She was interrupted by the ringing of the phone. Scott had seen only one telephone in the whole house, an elegant bone ivory antique in the hall.

Dr. Madison took a step forward, her hand on her chest. Her expression was a mixture of fear and excitement. "Oh dear," she said softly.

"Isn't anyone going to answer that?" Coulter asked.

"You don't understand." Dr. Madison turned to them. "That phone is merely for show. There are no working telephones at Booth House because the house has never been connected to the telephone lines. This is impossible."

39

"**W**ell, someone should answer it," Coulter said.

Jane folded her arms. "Don't look at us, you guys are the professionals."

"I'll do it," Anjali said. "Maybe I can get an idea of who we're dealing with." She quickly went across the hall and picked up the phone. "Hello?"

Girlish giggles filled her ears and then began to chant. "Ring around the roses, ring around the roses. You'll all fall down," they said in unison.

Scott came up behind her and laid his hand on her shoulder. "What do you hear?"

"Randall's twins, I think. They were singing a nursery rhyme and it couldn't have been creepier if Linda Blair was doing the chorus."

She was about to put the phone down when a soft fe-

male voice came through the receiver. "Help me . . . help."
The voice cut right to her insides. She reached up and
gripped Scott's hand.

And then silence once again.

"Another voice broke through," she said.

"Who?" Scott asked.

Slowly, she replaced the receiver and turned to find
everyone crammed into the doorway staring at her. "I
don't know, but she wants help."

Dr. Madison sighed. "The poor tormented dear, she's crying out for help. It has to be Molly. She needs us."

"I can't confirm—" Anjali began.

"But it makes perfect sense. Don't you see? Molly's guilt
has trapped her in the house." Dr. Madison came forward
and took Anjali's hands in hers. "She's reached out to you,
my dear. Jane, start setting up in here please. I can't wait
to get started."

Anjali went to Scott. "Can I talk to you privately?"

He opened the door to the kitchen. "No one's in here."

Once they were alone, she brought up what was bother-
ing her. "It's Dr. Madison, she's hell-bent on this presence
being Molly, but I don't think it is."

"I don't think it's Molly either. It just seems too tidy.
Anything else come to you?"

One of his rolled-up shirtsleeves was undone. She
moved closer and began folding it up. "I sensed an older female."

"Randall's wife?"

Without any conscious effort, her fingers trailed down
the inside of his arm and lightly touched his wrist. "Sarah?
I can't be sure."

When he didn't answer, she glanced up. His eyes were on her face. She looked down to where she was openly caressing his wrist. Startled, she let go of him.

"There you are!" Dr. Madison danced a little jig. "We're all set up. Come on."

They were in the dining room. Jane was using a handheld camera, Steve was operating the boom, and Darryl, the lighting guy, had brightened the room considerably. Anjali, Scott, Coulter, and Dr. Madison were sitting at the table.

"No séances," Anjali said firmly before Dr. Madison opened her mouth.

"But my dear, how else will we contact Molly?"

"Séances open the door too far, I—I just can't . . ."

"I have another idea," Scott said and placed a pad of paper and a pen in front of Anjali. "Has everyone heard of automatic writing?"

Jane smiled at him from behind the camera lens. "Why don't you explain it for the audience?"

"Normally automatic writing is when you ask a question, and then let your hand move across the page, writing whatever comes into your mind. But in Anjali's case, as a telepath, she'll ask the spirit a question and begin writing, waiting for the spirit to answer."

"Oh goody," Dr. Madison said eagerly. "Let's begin."

Anjali picked up the pen. "What do I ask and to whom do I ask it?"

"Be general," Scott said. "Ask the house what it wants."

"Just a casual chat," she said and picked up the pen. "Whoever you are? What do you want?" She began scrawling across the page, not writing words, just swirls of the pen line after line.

She reached the bottom of the page, turned it over, and started again. In seconds she had reached the bottom of that page and started on another page. After she had filled up five pages of scrawls, she looked up. "Absolutely nothing."

"Turn around, Angel," Coulter said quietly.

She turned to see her name scrawled across the dining room wall in large letters.

"Oh my God," Jane said.

"How wonderful." Dr. Madison gasped. "Just like at the Borley Rectory."

"The house wants me?" Anjali said weakly.

Scott stared at the wall. "Ask another question."

Coulter reached out and took her hand. She was glad for the support. Taking a deep breath, she asked, "Who are you?"

Slowly letters began to form under her name. M-O-L-L-Y.

"Are you getting this, Jane?" Dr. Madison asked.

"Damn straight."

Dr. Madison's eyes were bright, her cheeks flushed. "I was right. I knew we would contact Molly. After more than a hundred years, my dear, Molly has chosen to reach out to you."

"Personally I would have reached out to Angelina Jolie," Coulter drawled. Anjali shot him a dirty look and pulled away her hand.

For the next hour, the group had Anjali ask the spirit question after question, but no more words appeared on the walls.

"I think we should take a break," Scott said and stood.

Coulter yawned and stretched. "Fine by me."

Dr. Madison patted Anjali's hand. "Don't worry, dear. I'm sure Molly will contact us again."

"I'm not worried," Anjali began. "In fact—"

"So." Jane strolled to Scott's side and smiled up at him. "What's the plan?"

"Simple," Scott said. "We wait."

Rain pattered against the roof.

The house was bathed in darkness except for the sitting room, which was lit by the glow of the fire crackling in the fireplace.

Dr. Madison was asleep on the sofa.

Coulter, Anjali, Scott, and Darryl were playing poker by the fire. Between the three of them they already owed Coulter more than five thousand dollars.

Jane sat down next to them and took out a cigarette. She caught Anjali's eyes and with a sigh tucked it behind her ear. "Where's Scott?"

"Fold," Anjali said and put down her cards. "He wanted to do another walk-through." *And didn't ask for company.*

Jane leaned over and gazed at Steve's cards. "You're in. Ante up."

Steve folded instead. "I can't afford this."

"Neither can I," Darryl said and folded as well.

Coulter set down his cards with a flourish. "Read 'em and weep."

Steve's eyes widened. "I could've beat you!"

"Told you," Jane said and turned back to Anjali. "You haven't got dibs on him, have you? Your boss?"

"What? Scott?" Anjali asked.

"He's single," Coulter said, a mischievous glint in his eye. "Very available."

Jane grinned. "I did get that vibe."

Anjali couldn't decide whether she was more annoyed with Jane or with Coulter. She caught Coulter's eye. He was practically laughing at her. Okay, Coulter then. No wait. She was mostly annoyed at herself. Did she like Scott? What had happened in the kitchen? And did this place have a liquor cabinet?

The door to the parlor burst open. Scott strode in. "I need you guys to come with me upstairs. There's something you should see."

Anjali, Coulter, and Jane followed Scott up to the second floor. Darryl and Steve stayed behind with the snoozing Dr. Madison.

They entered the first bedroom to the left of the landing.

It was now in shambles.

Covers pulled from the bed. Furniture upturned. The vanity mirror hung at a crazy angle.

"What the hell happened?" Coulter asked.

"There's more," Scott said.

The remaining rooms on the second floor were in the same condition.

"The Booth family is not going to like this," Anjali said.

Scott checked the readings on the EMF, then looked up. "The Booth descendants rarely come by. A caretaker couple does the bare minimum to keep the place from falling to the elements."

"Something's happening," Coulter said. "I can feel it." He held out his hand, the fine hairs were standing up, the air was charged. Suddenly the door slammed shut.

Jane ran and tugged at the handle. "It won't open!"

"Hang on." Coulter stared at the door and focused. It flew open.

Darryl and Steve stood there, faces flushed, chests heaving. "What happened?" Darryl said. "We heard you calling us." He stared at Anjali.

"Me?"

"You were screaming for help," Steve said. "We came as fast as we could. The door wouldn't open and then"—he paused in wonder—"it did."

"I didn't call you," Anjali said and looked at Scott.

"Dr. Madison," he said.

They ran down the stairs, Scott in the lead. They burst into the sitting room. It was empty. Dr. Madison was gone.

40

"We have to split up," Scott said.

They were standing in the sitting room. Darryl and Steve wore identical expressions of guilt.

"It's not your fault," Anjali said. "It . . . they . . . she . . . whatever, used my voice. Creepy."

"We'll go in two groups and cover the house and the grounds," Scott instructed. "Everyone has each other's cell phone number, right?"

Coulter looked over at Steve's phone. "That's one tiny machine."

"I can bid on eBay with it," Steve said.

"Really?" Coulter moved in for a closer look. "Hey Wilder." He looked up. "What kind of crap did you give me?"

Scott ignored him. "If anyone gets into trouble, call."

"I think we should search the inside first," Anjali said.

Scott agreed. "I'll take two people with me to search out-side. You take the inside."

"I'm going with you," Jane said to Scott.

"Coulter, Jane, and I will take the grounds. Anjali, you, Darryl, and Steve take the house."

"Fine," Anjali said, trying to conceal her annoyance and not succeeding. Then again, she wasn't trying very hard. "But I don't see why we can't all search the house and grounds together?"

"It's faster this way," Scott said and left, Jane by his side.

Coulter hung back. "I did you a favor."

Anjali stared at him. "What?"

"You're jealous, aren't you? The first step is admittin' it. Now you know how you really feel about the guy so stop wasting time." He strolled off.

Darryl and Steve huddled together. "What do we do?"

Anjali sighed. "Shaggy, Scooby, come with me."

The grass was wet with mist and Coulter couldn't see hide nor tail of the exuberant Dr. Madison.

"Look," Scott said softly.

Ahead of them the carousel was slowly going round and round.

"Oh my God," Jane said and stepped closer to Scott, en-twining her arm with his.

Coulter walked up to the carousel and touched one of the horses as it went by. A soft energy flowed through him.

Anjali explored the third floor, followed by Darryl and Steve.

She could hear them whispering behind her. She

stopped in the middle of the hallway and they almost bumped into her. "What are you two whispering about?"

"Your boss and Jane," Steve said.

"Why?"

"Well, it keeps our minds off the fact that we're scared to death."

"I didn't sign up for this," Darryl said. "I'm just the lighting guy. I thought it was all going to be a big joke. Like the time Geraldo tried to raise the *Titanic*. I'd rather be back in Iraq with a news crew."

"Flying bullets we understand," Steve said. "But writing on the walls? Voices that don't exist?"

"I hear ya," she said. "We'll do a quick search and then meet up with the others. In the meantime, tell me about Jane and my boss."

"Jane's definitely interested," Darryl said. "She's a wild one and she likes guys who are conservative, figures she can teach them a thing or two."

"The men love her cool façade," Steve said.

Anjali rolled her eyes.

"No, they do," Steve insisted as they moved down the hallway. "They find her exciting."

A quick but thorough examination of the rest of the floor proved futile.

But she did get to hear all about Jane's charming quirks and traits.

"She's a rising star in documentary filmmaking," Darryl said as they headed for the stairs. "And—"

A piercing male scream erupted from behind them.

Anjali whirled around. "Where's Steve?"

Darryl's face was white with fright. "He was right behind us. Steve!"

Anjali raced back the way they'd come and found Steve staggering out of the last bedroom. "Pain," he gasped. "So much pain."

She grabbed him by the shoulders. "Are you okay? What happened?"

"Blister on my foot . . . popped . . . just now."

Darryl shoved him hard. "Christ! You're a jackass!"

Anjali let out a deep breath and counted to three. "I'm going downstairs. Do you want to sit down, Steve?"

"I can walk," he said and began limping after them.

A half hour had passed, and Scott, Coulter, and Jane still hadn't located Dr. Madison.

They were heading back up to the house when Scott saw Anjali crossing the lawn toward the carousel, trailed by Darryl and a limping Steve.

Scott sped up, realized Jane was still holding on to him, and reluctantly pulled her along. Coulter jogged after them.

Anjali had her hand on the carousel. "The twins, can you feel them?"

"Definitely," Coulter said.

"What happened inside?" Scott asked.

Anjali looked at him and then down to where his arm was entwined with Jane's. Scott quickly untangled himself. "Mrs. Booth is in the house, not Molly," she said. "I mean, she was in the house. I set her to rest."

"We saw it," Darryl said. "There was this loud sobbing and then the room became warm."

"Get it on film?" Jane asked.

"We got it," Steve said. "Anybody have a Band-Aid?"

"The twins have been playing with us all along then," Scott said.

Anjali nodded. "Pretending to be Molly." She frowned and looked toward the lake. "Something's there." She began walking toward the water.

Coulter and Scott followed behind her. They walked down the grassy bank, and Anjali veered right and began wading through a clump of waist-high bushes. She stopped and stared at the ground.

They ran to her side. Lying in the middle of the bushes was Dr. Madison.

After a hot cup of tea with lots of sugar, Dr. Madison was her usual perky self and absolutely thrilled she'd almost been the victim of a haunting. "I heard the girls calling to me down by the water. I was so excited, I started running. I must have fallen."

According to Anjali, Mrs. Booth shot her husband, Randall. Even after his affair with Molly resulted in the death of their daughters, Randall still continued with his philandering and took up with another woman just one year later.

Jane, Darryl, and Steve readied themselves in the dining room to film the removal of the twins' spirits.

It made for great TV.

Coulter kept the twins from distracting Anjali. Furniture moved, writing appeared on the walls, temperatures dropped, but in the end the twins slipped through the gap.

Afterward, Dr. Madison opened a bottle of champagne and a bottle of sleeping pills and passed both around.

Scott went outside to phone Eddie and tell him the news and when he came back, Anjali was gone.

"She's gone to get some sleep," Coulter said. "She took one of the doctor's pills."

41

She lay on her back staring up at the ceiling.

It was almost two and Anjali was wide awake.

She flung back the covers and decided to see if Dr. Madison was awake and could give her a pill. She'd decided not to take the other one and returned it.

Stupid move.

She pulled on a thin cotton robe over her sleeveless nightgown and slipped out of the room.

Dr. Madison's room was down the hall, and she quietly turned the knob, peeking inside. One of the small bedside lamps was on, and she could see by the soft glow that the woman was sleeping peacefully. Anjali decided to do a quick check for the pills.

The door opened behind her and Scott poked his head

in. He didn't seem surprised to see her. "I thought I heard you," he said.

Heard her? She knew for a fact that she hadn't made a bit of noise. "Did you have your ear pressed to the door or something?"

He entered the room, quietly shutting the door behind him. He was wearing a faded Stanford T-shirt and flannel pajama bottoms. "Are you angry with me?

"No," she said angrily.

"Yes you are and I want to know why."

"Can we have this conversation somewhere else?"

"Why are you mad at me?"

"I'm not mad. Besides, why do you care? You went off with Jane. The two of you scampering across the lawn, arm in arm."

"I've never scampered in my life and I'm not interested in Jane." He moved closer to her. "I thought you had a thing for Coulter."

"Everybody has a thing for Coulter."

"Do you?"

"No, I don't."

Scott reached out and took her hand, entwining his fingers with hers. Behind them, Dr. Madison snorted and turned over in her sleep.

He slid his hands up until he was holding her by the soft part of her arms. "You know how I feel about you."

"I don't make a habit of reading your mind."

He wrapped her in his arms. "You've done it before."

Her arms slid around his waist, and she pressed her cheek against his chest. "I have not."

"Well, I'll tell you then. I like you, Anjali."

"More than Nana Wilder?"

She could feel him smile. "Definitely more."

His fingers stroked her cheek before sliding under her chin and tilting her face up. She closed her eyes, and his mouth was on hers.

His mouth was much warmer than his hands.

She wrapped her arms around his neck and pulled him closer. And his lips went from warm to hot and he deepened the kiss until he might as well have been sucking the air from her lungs.

He was sweet and gentle and so warm that all she wanted to do was crawl inside him.

Dr. Madison giggled in her sleep, and Anjali pulled away. "Scott."

"Hmm?" He was kissing her neck.

"Dr. Madison?"

Instead of answering, he started kissing her again. It took every ounce of effort she had to tear her lips away. "We should go." She wasn't going to continue making out with Dr. Madison's snoring nearby.

Scott eased open the door. She slid past him, took hold of his hand, and pulled him down the hallway and into her room.

The door was barely shut when he wrapped her in his arms, holding her so tightly, she felt the breath escape her lungs.

She reached up and kissed him hard. And then eased back and rubbed his bottom lip with her thumb. "Sorry, did that hurt?"

"I don't know. Do it again."

Smiling, she nuzzled her face against his shoulder. "I need to catch my breath."

She could feel his lips against her hair as his hands slid inside her thin robe.

"I was jealous of Rhett Uglee," he murmured in her ear as his hands continued their caress. "When you started seducing him."

"I was not seducing him. I was pretending to be interested so his dead lady friend would show up."

He laughed softly, and she slid her hands into his thick hair.

And then she kissed him hard.

She had her breath back.

And she didn't want to waste it talking.

42

Relax, Anjali told herself, blinking in the bright lights the camera crew had set up. It's a public access station. Not CNN.

Seated diagonally across from her in one of the parlor's Windsor chairs, Coulter was more than relaxed. He was having the time of his life.

She watched as he smiled straight into the camera. "Actually, Diana, I didn't realize I could move people with my mind until a cute but crazy lesbian attacked me with a gun."

Diana Moss, the elegant blond features reporter for the local San Francisco morning show *Wake Up San Francisco*, kept her eyes trained on Coulter. "Well, you know what they say; a man's greatest asset is his mind."

Coulter's lips curved in an easy smile. "And mine is bigger than most."

Scott cleared his throat, straightened his tie, and leaned forward. "What Coulter *means* to say is that studies have shown that psychics, people with ESP, use a part of their brain that is closed to most. The ability is present in every human being; the reason why some can access it and the rest of us cannot is a mystery."

Diana managed to move her gaze from Coulter to Scott. "I see."

Anjali didn't think she did.

"Now, guys, let's talk tough." Diana cocked her head to the side and narrowed her eyes in what Anjali thought was a bad imitation of Barbara Walters. "You've solved a number of cases. Your last case—the Booth House in Pacific Grove—will be airing on the SciFi Channel. The producers of the piece vouch for you. But for most of us, when we hear the word psychic, we think con artist."

Anjali sensed a slight stiffening in Coulter at the last word.

"I don't blame you," Scott replied. "Most psychics are frauds."

"And how do we know that you aren't one of them?" Diana argued.

"Because," Coulter drawled, "we can prove it. You first, Angel."

Diana looked down at her cards. "Anjali Kumar? Now, you're empathic, right? You can read people's thoughts, their emotions?"

Anjali looked down at her hands. "Right."

Diana smiled challengingly. "Can you tell me what I'm thinking?"

Anjali looked up and focused on her.

How is this supposed to make me look like a serious journalist? Next thing you know I'll be interviewing Bigfoot.

Anjali's smile was cool. "I don't think you can get Bigfoot. I hear he's doing Conan."

Diana's mouth dropped open. "Oh my . . . I was just thinking that! I was! Now wait . . . what else am I thinking?"

Anjali took a moment and then gazed at her in disbelief. "Your favorite movie is *Showgirls*?"

Diana sat back in the chair and waved her notes like a fan. "Wow!"

"Ah . . . we're still rolling," the cameraman said after a few moments.

Diana sat up. "Right." She turned to Scott. "Now what exactly is your gift?"

Scott looked annoyed. "I don't have one."

"Too bad." Diana's gaze moved from Scott to Anjali. "Do any of you see dead people?

Anjali almost raised her hand. "I can't see them but I can communicate with them."

Coulter grinned. "She's like some cosmic umbilical cord to the spirit world."

Anjali thought about putting that catchphrase on a business card.

Diana's eyes widened. "Do you . . . are you talking to the dead right now? Because my uncle Joseph passed away unexpectedly and his estate is in probate hell and—"

"No," Anjali said quickly. "It doesn't work like that, at least not for me. I can't speak for other psychics, of course, but dead people don't come knocking. Their spirits are usually tied to a place."

"I see. Is there a way for us to know if those we care about are at peace? If they miss us?"

"I don't know," Anjali said. And that was the honest truth. Just because she was psychic didn't mean she was privy to any sort of privileged information like, say, Moses or Mohammed. She didn't know if there was a heaven or a hell, a nirvana or a celestial Playboy Mansion filled with large-breasted virgins.

Diana and the cameramen were all looking at her, disappointment etched into their faces. She tried to think of something upbeat. "Listen, none of you needs a psychic to tell you how a departed loved one feels. Only you can know that. Look in your heart. If someone special in your life has passed on and you miss them, it stands to reason that they miss you too."

Diana smiled. "I've never heard it expressed quite like that. I like your point. Although I doubt some of the celebrity psychics would agree."

"I could care less."

Diana looked at her thoughtfully. "Okay, I can't resist. I have to ask. Recently, a very well-known psychic was on a talk show and she said the End of Days is near. She predicted the Apocalypse. Your thoughts?"

Anjali shook her head in disgust. "This is why psychics get a bad name. Apparently, we can predict global catastrophes but can't tell you if it's going to rain next Monday."

Diana laughed. "I have wondered about that."

Anjali sat forward. "I believe there are certain things in life we are not meant to know the answers to. Is there a God? How was the universe created? How old is Dick Clark? And when is the world going to end?"

Scott winked at her and she sat back, smiling.

"I understand," Diana said. She turned to Coulter and smiled. "Now Mr. Marshall, if you don't mind? How about a little show?"

Coulter rubbed his hands. "Right. And I thought I was just gonna sit here and look pretty." His eyes moved around the room, then came to rest on the chair Diana was sitting in.

It began to move.

Diana was clueless until the cameraman gasped. By the time she looked down, her chair had risen four inches. She cried out. "Oh my God!"

"Coulter." Scott pointed to the floor, indicating he should cease and desist.

Slowly the chair lowered until it was touching the ground. There was a moment of hushed silence, and then Diana and the cameraman began clapping.

It wasn't exactly the thunderous applause of Madison Square Garden, but Anjali could tell Coulter was pleased. He jumped out of his chair and bowed.

At the very least, she thought, Coulter was good for ratings.

43

A month had passed since the Booth House case.

The Sci Fi Channel special was set to air in two days but early buzz, Dr. Madison's word of mouth, and Eddie's gruntwork had assured that the firm's phone was on a steady ring. Not just cases—big and small—but interviews with national and foreign publications.

Scott and Eddie were in the den having a drink when Eddie picked up the remote and turned the TV on, flipping channels until he stopped on *Crossing Over with John Edward*.

"Why do you watch this?" Scott demanded.

Eddie grinned. "He makes me laugh."

"People tune in to see this guy, then turn around and act skeptical over our *Wake Up San Francisco* appearance," Scott said. "It's frustrating."

"Blame it on Hollywood," Eddie said. "We've seen Spider-Man swing through Manhattan on a web. Keanu Reeves contort his body and dodge bullets, a nuclear explosion taking out Baltimore, so when we see people moving things with their mind, we think it's all special effects."

"But what about Anjali and mind reading?"

"That's easy," Eddie said. "No one will ever believe it's possible until it happens to them."

"So Anjali has to read the mind of every person in the United States?"

"Pretty much."

The front door opened and closed with a bang. Quick footsteps came down the hall and Anjali entered the room. Scott stood up feeling the same jolt of pleasure he always did when he saw her. She was wearing a lacy brown skirt and a silky multicolored sleeveless top.

"Hey guys," she said with a smile and hugged Scott.

"So how'd it go?" he asked.

Anjali's parents were in town and she'd shown them the Sci Fi special advance copy.

"They were impressed," she said. "I think my dad's finally coming around. Then again, he's on blood pressure medicine and needs to remain calm."

Scott laughed and sat back down. Anjali curled up next to him. "Where's Coulter?"

"Getting ready for his date," Scott said. "How's your sister doing?"

"Well, Vijay found out about her secret crush on Coulter and they're in marital counseling. But let's talk about something else." She smiled at Eddie. "What are you up to on this lovely Saturday night?"

"You know the owner of that shop in Union Square—the Psychic Tea Leaf? Well, I asked her out to dinner and she accepted."

"So Eddie got his groove back," Coulter said walking into the room.

"You look great," Anjali said. "You should wear black more often."

Scott decided he'd take Coulter apartment hunting tomorrow.

"Do we have any pizza left, Wilder?"

"I think you finished it."

"Damn, I'm starving." Coulter flopped down in the recliner, running his hands through his shower-damp hair.

"Don't you have dinner plans?" Anjali asked. "You're going to spoil your appetite."

"Impossible."

"I hear you're going out with the lovely reporter Diana Moss," Eddie said.

"We're going to some fancy restaurant for dinner and then to a party at Robin Williams's house."

"I want all the details," Anjali said. Coulter lifted his brow, and she quickly clarified, "I mean about the party!"

Coulter sat back and folded his arms across his flat stomach. "Don't worry, Angel, I'll give you *all* the details."

Anjali giggled.

Scott looked at her and she quickly cleared her throat.

Eddie grinned at Scott. "So you guys staying in?"

Anjali entwined her fingers with Scott's.

"Yes," he said.

*   *   *

Unfortunately, after a quick but very thorough kiss on the sofa, Scott put Anjali to work. She'd worn the silky camisole that gathered under the bust for nothing.

She was in the office staring at the computer screen. *Spectral Digest* magazine wanted a five-hundred-word essay from her on the pros and cons of being a telepath.

Pro, she wrote, *knowing the punch line of a joke before it's even told*.

Con, I feel dead people.

Scott set a glass of red wine for her on the desk and read what was on the screen. She could hear the amusement in his voice. "I'm not sure that's the angle they're going for."

"I have writer's block."

"I can help you with that."

She swiveled in her chair and stood up, resting her hands on his chest, her voice seductive. "You can?"

"I'll write up some points and you can fit them into the article."

She frowned. Sometimes Scott was too literal. She picked up the wineglass and took a big sip. She was going to take another when he took the glass from her hand and laid it back on the desk. His hands gently cupped her face. "Or we could talk about work later," he said.

That was the thing about Scott, he was a fast learner.

She was distracted for the next fifteen minutes or so, what with Scott pressing her up against the desk, one hand under her blouse, the other moving up her bare leg, pushing up her skirt. So she didn't feel the presence at first.

But then the goose bumps came.

An icy finger traced down her spine and she was cold.

Scott pulled back and rubbed her arms. "You're freezing."

"Something's here," she whispered.

His hands tightened just as all the lights turned off, plunging them into darkness.

Slow, shuffling footsteps sounded down the hall.

"Do you hear that?" she asked. "Footsteps?"

"I don't hear anything," he said. "Let me get the flashlight."

Anjali held onto him. "Stay here. It's outside the door."

He kept one arm around her and with the other dug in one of the desk drawers. He pulled out a flashlight and switched it on. The light jumped from corner to corner. "I don't see anything," he whispered.

"I do."

A man stood in the doorway dressed in a military uniform. A dead man. He was young, probably in his early twenties when he died.

Anjali felt light-headed. She was going to faint.

Scott pulled her against him. "Take a deep breath. I'm here."

She grabbed on to his shirt with both hands and tried to focus. So she'd never had a ghost actively seek her out before. No need to treat it any differently. Same rules applied.

"I'm going to throw up," she said.

"Don't look at it," Scott said. "Look at me. Tell me what's happening."

"He's standing in the doorway. He is . . . or was, a soldier." She couldn't help it. She had to look back. The ghost of the young man stared back at her with an expression so sad and defeated she felt her fear leave her.

Well most of it anyway.

She let go of Scott and took a step toward the door. *What do you want?* she asked. *Why are you here?*

He spoke and though she saw his lips move, it was as if his voice was inside her head. *You must stop it.*

"Stop what?" she said aloud. Scott looked from the doorway back to her.

The voice thundered in her head. *The evil in the desert!*

She cried out and clapped her hands to her ears. A gust of dry hot wind swept through the room.

The ghost of the soldier was gone.

Scott was sitting on the sofa, Anjali cradled against him.

If it hadn't been for her body turning cold, the lights going out, and the sudden wind, he wouldn't have thought anything was happening. And that disturbed him.

Spirits were tied to a location. They did not come calling. Even if certain movies suggested otherwise.

"Why are ghosts always so ambiguous?" Anjali asked.

"I don't have any reference for this. I need to talk to Eddie."

She looked up at him. "You don't know? I think I'm going to faint."

"I hate that I don't know this. He looked like a soldier?"

"Don't ask me if he was army or navy."

"I can't imagine what it must have been like . . . seeing him."

"I hope this isn't the start of a new trend. Feeling them is one thing, but if they start showing up here, at my apartment or the 7-Eleven."

"I think your local 7-Eleven will be spirit free."

"Why? Doesn't anyone haunt a 7-Eleven? Wouldn't they be attracted to the mummified hot dogs?"

He rubbed his cheek against her hair. "We'll figure this out."

"I hope so."

44

The call came the next morning.

Scott and Eddie were in the library, going through all the reference books trying to find more information on apparitions seeking out the living, when the phone rang.

Eddie answered and immediately opened his laptop and began typing, the phone cradled under his chin.

Scott got up and went to stand behind Eddie's chair. What he saw on the screen made him lean forward. Eddie had pulled up the website for a military facility—Blaine Air Force Base.

According to the site, the base was scheduled to open the beginning of next year in California's Yucca Desert.

The ghost of a soldier.

Eddie put down the phone. "You won't believe this. At a

time when our government is closing military bases all over the world, the one they spend hundreds of millions building turns out to be—"

"Haunted."

"They want us to fly down to Yucca and get briefed by an official."

Scott leaned back against the desk so he was facing Eddie. "Have you ever heard of anything like this? An apparition traveling hundreds of miles to deliver a premonitory warning? A warning that comes true?"

"Remember when I told you Vivica was involved in work with the government?"

"Don't tell me, this is it?"

"No, but thanks to those same contacts she'll be in Yucca too." At Scott's grimace, he grinned. "What can I say? It's a small field. You're bound to run into the same people again and again."

"I hear that the guys who study Mongolian throat singing have the same problem." Scott pushed off the desk and started pacing. "When do they want us there?"

"Two days. Every day that base stays closed is another gazillion dollars down the toilet."

The front door slammed shut and Coulter and Anjali's voices sounded in the hallway. "In here," Scott called out.

"Nothing like a calorie-loaded champagne brunch to take the edge off a visit from a dead man," Anjali said by way of greeting. "And I got to hear all about Coulter's date last night. Turns out Robin Williams does a real funny Johnny Carson bit where he puts on a turban and pretends to be psychic. And Diana Moss can't seem to enjoy a man without tying him up first."

Coulter pushed back his Stetson. "We're goin' out again tonight. Some pizza and light bondage, I reckon."

Anjali looked from Scott to Eddie. "What's wrong?"

"We've discovered something," Scott said and told them about the military base.

Anjali went over to the computer screen and studied the website. "Have there been any . . . deaths?"

"They wouldn't release any information," Eddie said. "But based on last night—"

"There have been," she finished. "So when do we leave?"

Scott touched her shoulder. "Are you sure about this?"

"When a dead man comes from God-knows-where to ask you a favor, I think you should listen."

The Blaine military base would soon be home to thousands of air force officers and their families. The possible haunted activity, however, was limited to the Flight Control Center—the pearl of the oyster.

Vivica hated the desert. She found the wide openness oppressive. She was a city dweller through and through. But the desert wasn't responsible for her irritation that morning. It was seeing Wilder, Eddie, and two people whose names she couldn't bother to remember sitting across from her at the conference table.

Oh wait, the remarkable specimen of masculinity was Coulter. Men that beautiful had only one working organ, though, and it was south of the pelvis.

She supposed the woman in their group was pretty enough, but she was short. Vivica didn't care for short people.

There was something going on between the woman and Wilder though. Vivica could tell by the way he was looking at her. Once he'd looked at Vivica like that.

Twisting open the cap of her water bottle, she leaned close to Maddox. "Hans is suitably restrained in the hotel room, is he not?"

Taking a cue from Dr. Frankenstein, Vivica had discovered that classical music had a remarkable soothing effect on Hans.

So did large doses of chlorpromazine and strong restraints.

Maddox nodded. "Schubert and straps."

The double doors to the conference room opened and a sturdy-looking woman with a head of short gray hair and a trim athletic figure entered the room, flanked by two military escorts.

Lieutenant Ann Jacobs, their military liaison on the case.

She walked up to the podium, leaving the two officers standing at attention on either side of the door.

Vivica turned her full attention to the front of the room.

"Ladies and gentlemen," the lieutenant began in a firm, no-nonsense voice. "On behalf of our country's government, I want to thank you for coming today. This is a highly unusual situation and we appreciate your expertise. As you know, this is a secret information briefing. I trust that the details will not leave this room." A small smile played around her lips. "Although we weren't very successful at keeping Roswell a secret, now were we?"

Across the room Scott's team was all grins and soft laughter. Maddox looked at Vivica and murmured. "Am I supposed to laugh?" Vivica shrugged and forced a polite smile.

"Let me give you the big picture," Lieutenant Jacobs said. "The military has put a billion dollars into a state-of-the-art property that is inoperable. We need it up and running. This base is integral to national security and it's gathering dust."

Vivica wanted to interject a question but the lieutenant had asked that all questions and comments be held until the end of the briefing. She scribbled on the legal pad in front of her and noticed Scott and Eddie doing the same.

"To reiterate," the lieutenant continued. "The purpose of this briefing is to bring you up to date on the number of strange occurrences that have plagued construction of the Flight Control Center from the beginning. We're talking equipment malfunction, power outages, theft of materials from the site along with personal belongings of the engineers and workers. The real trouble started with the moodiness and personality changes of the crew. Tempers were unusually high on the site. People were sensitive to the slightest look or comment. Fights broke out on a routine basis. One of our top engineers was removed from the base due to a nervous breakdown.

"We've had officers stationed inside the center around the clock. When the morning shift arrived they found one of the night officers dead—shot by his shift partner. The shooter had no memory of committing the act. I'll spare you the details of the subsequent interrogations and psych evaluations. Suffice it to say that we all agreed to a plea of temporary insanity. And now I'll open it up to questions."

"Lieutenant Jacobs," Scott began. "Have—"

"Have you found pockets of unusual electrical discharge?" Vivica asked. "Power bursts?"

The lieutenant nodded. "It's common to encounter power surges when wiring a new building, but the malfunctions we've experienced have been baffling. At this point we've given up trying to control the electrical problems."

Scott cleared his throat. "Did any one person seem to trigger the most occurrences? Serve as a catalyst?"

Lieutenant Jacobs smiled. "Like the little girl in *Poltergeist*?"

Coulter raised his hand. "That joke's been done before. By me."

The lieutenant stared at him, puzzled.

Vivica rolled her eyes and whispered under her breath. "Bloody clown."

The lieutenant turned her attention to Scott. "To address your question, Mr. Wilder, wouldn't the officer who committed the shooting be considered a catalyst of sorts?"

"Not exactly," Scott said. "He was definitely affected, as was the discharged engineer, but I wouldn't classify either as a catalyst. Their personalities, life experiences, and genetic makeup made them more susceptible to the environment. I'm looking for someone who always seemed to be around when the strange events occurred—whether they appeared affected or not."

"In that case," Lieutenant Jacobs said, "the only catalyst I can think of—"

"Is the building," Vivica finished. "The Flight Control Center. This isn't a case of accidental PK activity, Wilder."

"PK?" the lieutenant asked.

"Psychokinesis," Eddie answered with a smile. "We can lapse into jargon—or nerd speak—now and again."

Lieutenant Jacobs smiled back. "My ex-husband used to

complain he had to dodge flying jargon whenever there was a dinner party at the base."

Eddie's smile widened.

Vivica drummed her fingers on the table impatiently. Eddie and the lieutenant could go have middle-aged sex in the back of a jeep for all she cared. But for now she wanted answers. She held up a finger. "If we could get back to the Q and A?"

"Of course," Lieutenant Jacobs said briskly.

"I'm wondering about specific physical manifestations like vapors, clouds of smoke?"

"Yes, Dr. Bates, we've had reports of black clouds of smoke that would appear randomly and dissipate just as quickly. What with the shooting and other major occurrences, that detail was left out of the official report."

Scott looked at Eddie and then Vivica. "Ectoplasm?"

Even though she hated to agree with him, she nodded. "That's my guess."

"Ectoplasm?" the short woman sitting next to Scott said. "As in, I got slimed?"

Vivica rolled her eyes again.

"Define ectoplasm," the lieutenant said. "I'm afraid, like Ms. Kumar, that my only reference is *Ghostbusters*."

"There's an ectoplasm cocktail." Coulter leaned back in his chair and fixed his blue gaze on Vivica. "Lots of vodka, some Grand Marnier, and it's got a kick like a mule."

"How illuminating," she replied and turned to the lieutenant. "Ectoplasm is a force of dense bio-energy liberated during psychokinesis. A sort of teleplasmic mass."

"English please?" Lieutenant Jacobs said.

Eddie responded. "The stuff that oozes out of ghosts and makes it possible for them to do the stuff they do, like move furniture, scare the crap outta you, etc."

"Now I get it. Thank you, Dr. Mirza."

Vivica curled her lip.

"Ectoplasm isn't always slimy either," Scott said. "Appearance varies. One of its forms, though, is vaporous— gray, black, or white in color. Think of a self-propelled cloud of smoke, moving at its own speed, never losing denseness."

The lieutenant shook her head in wonder. "This is a lot to process. I happily admit to being out of my element here, but I can offer a suggestion. Why don't we visit the site?"

Scott held up his hand. "Wait. I want to know more about these personality changes. I'd like to talk to the engineer who was relieved of his duties."

Vivica frowned. "The personality shifts are incidental, Wilder. They could be caused by anything, the desert heat, work stress. I want to see firsthand what we're dealing with."

Scott faced her. "Look, I want to get in there as much as you, but I can't forgo the safety of my team until I know more."

"Well bully for you, but I appreciate the military's need for urgent action."

"How about a compromise?" Lieutenant Jacobs said. "I agree; precautions need to be taken. I'll have my aide bring up the engineer's information." She looked down at her watch. "It's oh-nine hundred now. I'm scheduling a tour for sixteen hundred hours."

"What the hell time is that?" Coulter asked. "Do I add twelve? Multiply?"

Vivica stood up. "Four P.M. We'll be there."

The lieutenant gathered up her papers and smiled at all of them. "To reiterate, the Department of Defense appreciates both your teams' expertise on this . . . unusual matter. You're the best in the field, and we're counting on you for a quick resolution. It will be looked upon most favorably, I assure you."

"She means more than just a thank-you, right?" Coulter asked.

46

Both groups assembled promptly at four o'clock in front of the Flight Control Center—a two-story wonder of steel and glass.

Anjali was relieved when Vivica showed up with just Maddox in tow.

"Where's your trained psycho, Vivica?" Coulter asked. "The one who's sharp as a mashed potato and makes the rest of us feel safe?"

"This is just the rehearsal," Vivica said coolly. "Hans will be ready when I need him."

Lieutenant Jacobs arrived in a sedan with two officers. Anjali reflected that in a desert with high temperatures of 119 in August, one didn't want to be tooling around in an open military jeep.

And then they were entering the center.

The moment she stepped inside, a wave of dizziness hit Anjali. She leaned back against the wall as the room began to tilt.

"What's wrong?" Scott demanded. Behind him, Coulter and Eddie watched her with concern.

Anjali pressed a shaky hand to her face. "Just a dizzy spell," she said and pushed off the wall.

Scott looked skeptical.

She gave him a shaky smile. "I'm okay, really. Let's get this over with."

"I wish I could have spoken with that engineer," Scott said.

"You left him half a dozen messages," Eddie said. "He can still call back."

Their footsteps echoed through the empty building as they walked across the smooth white tile floor. Anjali thought about the dead soldier. So he'd been killed by a fellow officer, and possibly a friend. She was still unclear about his message. Had he been warning her to stay away from the base?—too late. Or did he want her to stop whatever was making people psycho in this place?

A set of instructions would have been nice.

Lieutenant Jacobs pointed out the damaged light fixtures. Coulter leaned up to touch one of them and the bulb sprang to life. He did the same with the next bulb over. The lieutenant and officers looked on in amazement.

The tour continued. "It's getting cold in here," Eddie said. Everyone else agreed.

Anjali touched her cheek. Her skin was warm. The whole place was warm.

She pulled her tank top away from her body and wished she'd worn shorts instead of jeans.

They left the entrance wing and headed down a long corridor of offices. None of the offices had doors installed yet and neither did any of the restrooms. As she passed by the second restroom, Anjali caught a glimpse of her face in the mirror.

She grabbed on to the door frame and stared at her reflection. She looked horrible. Her hair was dull and lank, the ends split and thin. Her skin had an unhealthy sheen, and there were dark hollows under her eyes and lines around her mouth.

"Angel, are you okay?" Coulter was touching her shoulder.

She brushed his hand away. "I'm fine, just thirsty."

"Here." Eddie handed her his bottle of water. "Do you still feel dizzy?"

"No." She took a quick sip and handed it back to him.

Ahead of them, Scott was talking to Lieutenant Jacobs. Catching Anjali's eye, he smiled.

Annoyed, she turned to Coulter and Eddie. "I just wish Scott would shut up so we could get on with the tour."

The sound of doors closing and voices from the floor above silenced everyone.

Coulter stated the obvious. "We're the only ones in here right?" Lieutenant Jacobs nodded.

"I want to see the upstairs," Vivica said.

Anjali lingered behind and looked in the mirror again. If anything, she looked even worse.

"Anjali?" Scott was calling her.

Irritation welled inside her. The man hovered around her like she was a child who needed constant supervision.

Scott was beside her, tilting her chin so he could look into her eyes.

She pushed his hand away. "I'm fine. I know I look hideous, but I'm fine."

She brushed by him and went to join the others.

Lieutenant Jacobs was talking. She swept her hand through the air. "This is where black clouds of smoke have appeared and gone."

Anjali blinked and tried to focus on the older woman. Where were they?

The last she remembered, she'd been walking away from Scott. Now she was on the second floor listening to the lieutenant.

She had no memory of how she'd gotten there.

Anjali's heart pounded. What the hell was going on? She grabbed the person next to her. "Wait. How did we get up here?"

Maddox stared at her, puzzled. "We took the stairs."

"Look!" Vivica pointed to a corner, where a black cloud of smoke began appearing. The air was foul and everyone covered his mouth and nose.

Anjali's dizziness returned with a vengeance. The room began a slow spin. Bile rose in her throat.

Panicking, she turned around and stumbled toward the stairs. She had one thought and one thought only.

I need to get out of here.

I need to get out right now.

Anjali was puking her brains out in the bushes and Scott was holding her hair back.

She straightened. "I think I'm done." She rinsed her

mouth out with water. Eddie handed her a stick of gum. "Thanks," she said.

As casually as possible, she glanced at her reflection in the side mirror of the lieutenant's car. She looked normal, a little drained, but normal.

"What the hell happened in there?" Coulter asked.

Before she could answer, the rest of the group exited the building and came toward them.

"Are you okay?" Lieutenant Jacobs asked.

She nodded. "But there's something powerful in that place. I didn't realize I was being . . . affected, until it had already happened." She looked at Scott. "It wasn't like that time on the ship. I wasn't aware of a presence inside me. Here, everything I was thinking and feeling seemed normal, like it was all coming from me. It wasn't until I ended up on the second floor with no memory of how I'd gotten there—"

Scott drew in a sharp breath. "You lost time?"

"I . . . I guess."

Eddie was watching Scott. "Lost time, unexplained anger?"

Vivica slowly nodded. "The black smoke accompanied by the foul smell."

Anjali looked at Coulter, who shrugged. She grabbed Scott's arm. "What is it?" The expression in his eyes frightened her. He looked unnerved.

"I can't say for certain. None of us can. But I think we're dealing with . . . an entity."

47

An hour later they were back in the conference room at the base.

"Is this entity removable?" Lieutenant Jacobs asked.

"Absolutely," Vivica said.

Scott disagreed. "There are no absolutes when it comes to dealing with an entity. This isn't a ghost. This isn't the spirit of someone who's died. This is a nonhuman, noncorporeal presence, and nobody knows where it comes from and what it's capable of."

Next to him Anjali murmured. "Maybe we should just bring in an exorcist?"

Scott reached over and squeezed her hand.

"What I can't understand," the lieutenant said, "and I don't pretend to have even an inkling about how to deal with this situation, is why only Ms. Kumar was affected and not Mr. Marshall?"

"Look at it this way," Eddie said. "Take two athletes—a swimmer and a quarterback. Both highly skilled, both classified under sports, yet both completely different in their talents and use of muscle groups."

"I hope I'm the quarterback," Coulter said.

Lieutenant Jacobs sighed. "I've spoken with the department. We need this situation dealt with ASAP. A certain congressional committee is demanding to know what we've done with the funds that were allocated to us. Come hell or high water, the chairman of the Joint Chiefs plans on paying the base a visit next week. Now if it was up to me, I'd close this place down for the next ten months or ten years, however long it took to make it safe. But I don't have the last word here."

Scott appreciated the woman's position and her candor, but his back was riled up just the same. Did the government think that by putting a deadline on something like this, it would automatically get done?

His jaw set, he made a decision. "We need more time. I want to talk to all the officers, construction workers, and engineers affected by being on this site, as well as witnesses to the events. He turned to Eddie. "The Anasazi shaman in New Mexico—"

"Has dealt with this before. I'll contact him right away."

"How much time are we talking about?" the lieutenant asked.

"More than we're getting," Scott said. "At least three weeks."

"That's not possible."

"It's what I'm offering." It pained Scott to think that his refusal to compromise might get his team kicked off the case. He could wait his entire life and not see anything like this again. He didn't need to see the restrained excitement on Eddie's face to know he felt the same way. Anyone in their field would. But going after whatever was out there without being fully prepared would be like hunting a great white shark armed with only a lobster fork.

Vivica looked at Scott like he was nuts. "What are you planning to do? Write a thesis on the entity first?" She smiled at the lieutenant. "My team and I will go into the center tonight. We'll be done by morning."

Lieutenant Jacobs looked taken aback. "By morning?"

"Yes."

"Well then, I was hoping for some sort of a consensus but . . . Dr. Bates if you can deliver, I can promise you enough funding to keep your research going for the next fifteen years."

"How much dinero we talkin' about?" Coulter asked.

The lieutenant looked amused. "A lot. Now, a team of officers will accompany Dr. Bates's team inside. Meanwhile, I need to inform the higher-ups of both your decisions. You know how to reach me." She left the room accompanied by two burly escorts.

"Vivica, really," Scott said. "What you're doing is dangerous."

"The available research points to the fact that an entity can be cast out."

"Not exactly, what the research *theorizes*—"

"We can argue semantics all day, Wilder. I have better things to do."

Eddie looked at her. "In all the years we've worked together, I've never known you to act this rash."

"In case you haven't noticed," Vivica said, "the university has pulled our department's funding. Parapsychology is still considered a joke science. We're at the mercy of private backing, and wealthy benefactors are few and far between."

"But to risk yourself and your—"

Vivica laughed. "Don't be so melodramatic, Mirza." Beside her, Maddox looked nervous. "Besides, you've seen Hans in action."

"Hans?" Anjali said. "You mean the man who attacked me on the *Santa Perla*? You can't handle him, Vivica. He'll be like a loaded gun in the entity's hands. He practically welcomes possession."

Vivica raised her brow. "So do you from what we witnessed today."

Anjali winced.

"Besides," Vivica added, "after you all *fled* the *Santa Perla* that night, Hans cleared it. I've worked extensively with him since then. And he'll cast out the entity."

"I'm afraid you're on your own then," Scott said.

Vivica stood up. "Oh dear, and I was so counting on your help."

Coulter turned to Scott as soon as Vivica had left. "You're just giving up? This is a huge deal! We could be big. We could be household!"

"As much as I'd like to be a popular cultural reference, I think not."

Coulter leaned forward. "We've handled pretty much everything till now as easy as a warm summer breeze. You reckon this is that much different?"

"Yes," Scott said.

Coulter looked at Eddie. "Come on, man."

"Scott's right," Eddie said. "We don't know enough about what's inside that place."

"So we're just gonna let this juicy little opportunity slip us by?"

Scott sighed. "I want this too, but on my terms."

Coulter exhaled in frustration. "What do you think, Angel? You fought it in there. I mean, what can this thing really do? Kill all of us? Come on."

"I just keep having visions of *The Shining*," she said. "What if it uses me against the rest of you? I don't want to end up chasing you through the center with an ax."

"Christ Almighty," Coulter said. "I don't know about ya'll but I don't plan on chasing ghosts for the rest of my life." He pushed back his chair and stood. "Normally, I'd think twice about putting my fate in Queen Vivica's hands. She isn't fit for a drunk man, much less a sober one. But this time, boss, she's right and you're wrong."

And with that he left.

48

Vivica waited at the entrance to the center with Maddox, Fitch, Gaspar, Hans, and two officers.

Coulter thought she didn't seem at all surprised to see him. "Well, well," she said, inspecting him from head to toe, "looks like Mr. Tall, Blond, and Country will be joining us."

"This is a one-time-only deal," Coulter said. "I don't want to catch whatever you have."

Amused, Vivica tossed him what looked like a cell phone. "Walkie-talkie. Military issue, can withstand shock, vibration, and temperature extremes. It's set on our frequency. Keep it on."

Coulter clipped it to his jeans and looked up to see Hans staring at him, his gray eyes wide and unblinking. "Keep that pasty white body away from me. You hear?"

Hans turned away.

"Let's do this," Vivica said and followed the officers into the center.

Coulter brought up the rear.

They checked every inch of the first floor and finally ended up in the large cafeteria. The lights weren't working and moonlight spilled from the windows, filling the room with shadows and illuminating the rows of empty tables and chairs.

"Hans, anything?" Vivica asked.

He shook his head.

Coulter looked at him. "Speak much?"

"It's better if he doesn't," Fitch said. "He's a little . . ." He made the crazy sign above his head.

"Temperature's dropping," one of the officers said. Coulter had almost forgotten they were there. They tended to just keep quiet and look stoic.

"Be alert," Vivica ordered. "And don't do anything stupid." Her gaze rested on Fitch.

The cold descended. Coulter let out his breath and watched it turn into a small puff of fog.

And then they heard it.

A loud crash deep in the building.

Hans stared up at the ceiling and pointed. "It's waiting."

Vivica cocked her head. "Listen."

Coulter heard it, a low sizzling sound. One by one all the lights flashed on and then turned off. "I can handle this," he said and focused. The bulb directly above him turned on and burst in a shower of sparks.

"Let me guess," Maddox said. "You can recharge 'em, you just can't fix 'em."

"It wants to come in," Hans whispered. "I won't let it come in."

"Good boy, Hans," Vivica said and patted his head.

"So how do we get rid of this thing?" Coulter demanded.

Vivica placed her hands on her hips and gazed around the room before stopping on him. "What's the best way to flush out your enemy?"

"No freakin' clue."

"We engage it."

49

The phone's ringing woke Anjali up.

She blinked a few times, adjusting to the dark of the room.

Beside her, Scott murmured into the phone. "What time? Nothing since then?" He hung up and softly cursed.

She sat up, pushing her hair back from her face. "What happened?" And then as realization dawned on her. "Coulter . . . the others?"

"Lieutenant Jacobs's men called in at eleven to touch base. She hasn't heard from them since or from anyone else."

"And what time is it now?"

"Three." Scott grabbed the phone and called Eddie,

quickly filling him in on the details. "Be ready in ten minutes," he said and hung up.

She sat there watching him get dressed. "You guys think you're going alone, don't you?"

He didn't answer, stepping into his shoes.

She yanked off the covers and grabbed her jeans and a shirt. "Have fun trying to keep me here."

He caught her face between his hands and kissed her hard.

"I'm going with you," she said against his lips.

"No."

She pulled away. "You think I'll pull a Hans and hurt someone."

Scott reached for his kit, which he always kept packed and ready to go. "You're nothing like Hans. The person I'm worried you'll hurt is yourself."

She stared at him for a long moment. "I adore you but you're an asshole."

He smiled. "So you tell me."

She began pulling on her jeans. "I'm going, you know. You can fire me if you want."

There was a loud knock at the door. She heard Scott open it as she pulled the shirt over her head.

"Good, you made it," he said, and she assumed he was talking to Eddie.

Until a tall, heavily muscled officer entered the room, practically having to duck his head just to clear the door.

"I'm going," Scott said. "She's staying."

Anjali moved toward him but the officer blocked her path. She stared up at him and then at Scott. "You've got to be kidding me!"

Scott was at the door. "Promise you'll never stop calling me an asshole," he said.

"Scott!"

She watched him leave in disbelief. "You bastard!"

A njali walked into the Flight Control Center.

Twenty minutes spent yelling at Lieutenant Jacobs about sexual discrimination, male chauvinism, and glass ceilings—Anjali figured the lieutenant had experienced all the above during her career—and the officer guarding her was called off.

All she had with her was a flashlight and a cell phone—nobody had bothered to pack a rocket launcher or some holy water.

Are you there, Vishnu? It's me, Anjali.

She'd barely taken a few steps when a powerful wave of dizziness struck her. She would have fallen to the floor if the wall hadn't been behind her.

Alien thoughts beat against the walls of her skull.

The entity. Invisible but powerful, like a toxic gas.

Okay, she'd expected this.

She closed her eyes and envisioned the dizziness as something solid she could just push out of her head, out of her body.

It worked.

Something to be said for sheer mental brute force.

Flickering lights bathed the interior of the center. The place was cold and she didn't see or hear anyone.

But they had to be in there. Unless they'd all run away and she was walking around like a fool while they were at the High Desert Inn bar getting drunk.

No, they were there—possibly possessed, possibly skulking around corners ready to pounce on her or dismember her or . . .

Stop it, she told herself. *You can't die now. You finally have a functioning relationship with your parents.*

The silence was absolute, falling heavy and thick around her shoulders.

She spoke too soon.

The sound of someone singing reached her ears. The voice was sexless, high-pitched and heavy at the same time. The words were unintelligible, but there was a tune, one she wouldn't want to whistle in the future.

She moved cautiously along one hallway after another, passing open doors and forcing herself to look inside and see if anyone was there.

Ten minutes after it began, the singing stopped. This time she heard footsteps, slow and methodical. Right behind her. She gripped her flashlight.

She held her position in the darkness. She knew she had to turn around, see what or who was there. She took a deep breath and swung around, the light from the torch bouncing down the passageway.

Empty.

What was up with demonic presences that wanted to play hide and seek like children?

She turned back around and started walking, swinging the flashlight back and forth like a blind man with a cane.

She'd gone no more than six or seven paces when the footsteps started again, this time moving toward her at a run. On pure instinct, she took off. Racing down the corridor. But her pursuer gained on her and slammed into her from behind. She fell, banging her knees painfully on the floor. The flashlight rolled away in a squiggle of light.

"I think I hit him!"

Anjali recognized the nasally tones of one of Vivica's minions.

"I'm not a him," she snarled. Crawling, she grabbed the flashlight and turned it on the man behind her.

It wasn't Maddox but one of the others. Fitch?

"What are you doing?" she snapped, standing up.

Another minion came to stand beside him. "We thought you were it," he said.

"Who? The entity?"

"It has a body now."

She felt sick. "Hans?"

Fitch's eyes were wide. "We don't know."

"Where is everyone?" she asked.

"We were all separated on the second floor," Gaspar said. "Fitch and I headed downstairs and started walking toward the entrance. We knew the way; it was impossible to get lost. But we couldn't find it. We couldn't find the way out."

"Everyone's dead," Fitch said.

"Dead?" Anjali croaked.

Gaspar nudged him and he shrugged. "Okay, maybe I'm exaggerating. We really don't know if everyone's dead. But I bet they're all servants of Lucifer now."

"I'll show you the door," she snapped. They huddled behind her as she retraced her steps.

At the entrance doors, Fitch and Gaspar shoved each other in their haste to leave.

"Hold it!" They turned around and she glared at them. "Tell Lieutenant Jacobs everything and make sure she sends in a fleet or whatever the hell the air force does. And," she added in a steely voice, "if I find out that you two ran off without doing what I just said, I will find you. You thought Hans was scary. You haven't seen what I can do."

They nodded and ran out the doors into the night.

Anjali found the two officers in one of the offices, huddled under a desk and whimpering about a monster. She led them out.

She found Maddox with a large gash on his forehead in the cafeteria. He drifted in and out of consciousness, and it took a long time to get him outside. She left him there, propped up against the building.

There were five more people still inside the center— Scott, Eddie, Coulter, Vivica, and Hans—and one more floor to check. She headed upstairs, trailing her fingers along the railing and periodically looking down into the atrium of the lobby in case she'd missed somebody.

The odd singing started up again when she reached the top, followed by a loud screeching noise like the tearing of metal.

Too late she turned and saw the heavy metal light fixture disconnect from the ceiling and swing toward her.

51

She was hanging by a thread.

Or rather by the railing.

Struggling, she tried to pull herself up when a hand reached down, grasped her arm.

She found herself staring into Hans's gray eyes as he hauled her to safety.

"The others," she asked. "Where are they?"

He started walking. Anjali followed him.

They were heading toward the back of the building. Seeming to sense their presence, office doors banged open and shut, open and shut with so much force, she felt as though she were walking through a battle with cannon fire.

Hans led her into a room that looked like an observation deck. If it had been daylight, she would have been able to see the runway. A few lights blinked from the myriad of computer screens and systems. Otherwise the room was pitch dark.

She swung the flashlight around and gasped. Scott lay on the floor surrounded by shattered lights and ceiling debris. She ran to his side. His eyes opened and widened at the sight of her. "What are you doing here?"

She stroked the hair back from his brow. "I've come to rescue you."

He tried to sit up and groaned. "I always did need saving."

"Are you badly hurt?"

"I want to say yes . . . but no, I'm not."

She helped him up and he leaned on her heavily, favoring his left side. "Eddie. His leg is bad."

"Where is he?"

Scott pointed to a dark corner near the door, and she swung the beam there. Eddie had his back against the wall, his legs trapped under an immense metal cabinet. "I couldn't move it," Scott said.

"Hans, can you help?" she asked.

Scott raised his eyebrows. "Hans?"

"He saved my life. Don't ask me why."

Hans moved closer to Eddie, and the cabinet creaked and began to move. Slowly, it lifted off his leg and returned to an upright position.

Anjali went to Eddie; Scott followed, limping.

The flashlight illuminated Eddie's bloodied leg and his gray-tinged complexion. "I knew there was a reason I didn't trust the government," he said. "I pay my taxes and for this?"

She touched his cheek. "Can you stand?"

"Not even if you paid me."

She looked around but didn't see Coulter. A cold feeling took root inside her. Her hand drifted to Eddie's shoulder, and she looked up at Scott. "Where's Coulter?"

The lights in the room came on. A whirring started up as the computers came to life.

Coulter stood in the doorway.

Or something that looked like Coulter.

He began to walk toward her. She froze. Beneath her hand, Eddie tensed.

The sharp sound of a gun being clicked broke the spell. Vivica stood behind Coulter, a gun trained on him. She looked wild, her eyes wide, the side of her face scratched, and took aim.

"No!" Anjali shouted. "Don't kill him!"

"That's the idea," Vivica said. "He dies, the entity goes with him. It's the only way."

"This was your brilliant plan, Vivica?" Scott said. "Let the entity possess a body and then kill it?"

"I thought Hans could cast out the evil, but Hans isn't being very obedient. So this is plan B. Can you think of a better idea? He has to die or that thing will kill us all."

She took aim, but the gun went flying out of her hand. An invisible force slammed her back against the wall. Her eyes rolled shut, and she slid to the ground.

"What do we do?" Anjali whispered.

"You have a connection with Hans," Scott said. "Together you might be able to cast that thing out."

Anjali stood and held out her hand. "Hans?"

He came to her and she reached out and gripped his hand. Then she closed her eyes. She could feel Hans in her head—only this time she didn't mind.

She reached out, trying to connect with Coulter.

Blackness surrounded her.

A giant void.

She could hear someone . . . Coulter screaming. It came from everywhere. Pouring out of his mind, into hers . . .

She tried the light. She envisioned the doorway, tried to push the entity through, but it was too strong.

Hans squeezed her hand. She opened her eyes and saw him. The dead soldier.

Hans was trying to tell her something and finally she understood. She gazed at the soldier, and he nodded.

It was the only way.

The soldier's spirit invited the entity in. Coulter slumped to the floor.

The entity was now tied to a human spirit. And she knew what to do with spirits.

She envisioned the doorway filled with light.

It took all of her and Hans's combined strength, but they pushed the spirit through.

The air grew warmer, and it was as if an unseen weight was lifted off the place.

Scott was kneeling beside Coulter. She crouched down beside them. "Coulter?"

He blinked at her. "What happened?"

She smiled. "You won't believe it, but Hans saved the day. Along with one strong-willed soldier."

"And a lot of help from Anjali," Scott added.

In the corner, Vivica moaned and lifted a shaking hand.

Anjali looked at Scott. "Should we . . . ?"

Scott gazed at Vivica for a long moment. "I think I'll go check on Eddie." Anjali watched him walk away.

"I'm confused." Coulter blinked several times. "Did you say something about Hans saving me?"

"Yup." Speaking of Hans, she wanted to thank him. She looked around the room but he was nowhere in sight. She closed her eyes and tried reaching out to him but it was no use.

He was gone.

From downstairs came the sound of booted feet hitting the floor. "The cavalry's arrived," Anjali said.

Coulter sat up and ran his fingers through his hair. "About damn time. I don't mean to sound unpatriotic and all but Uncle Sam and I are partin' ways."

"You didn't think this was an exciting adventure?" Anjali teased.

"Oh yeah," he murmured. "Better than cable."

52

"**S**cott, people are staring at me," Anjali said.

"No they aren't."

Anjali stared at the crowd of her relatives filling the Bombay Exchange restaurant for her cousin Simran's engagement party, and frowned. "Yes they are. Do you think they saw the article?"

The *Bay Area Sentinel* had published an op-ed piece about her. "Anjali Kumar: Psychic Guru or Quack?"

"Everyone knows the *Sentinel* is a tabloid," Scott reassured.

"I need a drink."

"You have one in your hand. We just came from the bar."

She did indeed have a vodka tonic in her hand and took a sip. "If anyone asks, this is Sprite."

"Your father is waving me over," Scott said. "Will you be able to handle any inquisitive aunts who come your way?"

She looked over to where her dad was standing with a group of her uncles and indeed motioning to Scott.

"Be prepared to give out some more stock tips," she warned.

"If only my own father were so easy to impress," Scott said and went to join her dad.

Anjali was thrilled her parents liked Scott. Sure he wasn't Indian, but he had an MBA from Stanford, owned a nice house, and drove a Range Rover. And as one of her aunties had informed her earlier at the party, "Good thing he's so fair. Your children will have nice complexions."

Scott was with her at the time, and Anjali thought she'd die a slow and painful death from embarrassment.

No one from Scott's family had made any such comments. She'd driven to Marin County to meet them, and pulling into the drive of their huge home in ultra-wealthy Belvedere, she'd felt like Gandhi taking on the British Empire.

Also because she'd fasted for days not wanting to look fat.

Either way they seemed to like her just fine.

Anjali downed the rest of her drink and headed for the restroom. She could feel her bindhi sliding down her forehead.

Unfortunately a woman stopped in Anjali's path and stared. "I read that article about you," she said. "Is it true?"

"That I'm a quack? No."

"But anyone who thinks they can . . ." The woman's voice trailed off as Zarina came up to them.

Her sister was wearing a pink sari. The gossamer material was embroidered in gold, and Zarina wore gold chandelier earrings and matching bracelets. Anjali had never seen her sister look so beautiful.

The look of annoyance she was familiar with.

Zarina glared at the woman and put her arm around Anjali. "She's not crazy. She's my sister."

Anjali's eyes widened, and she stared at Zarina in amazement.

"I never said . . . oh who cares." The woman sniffed and walked away.

Anjali hugged her sister. "You mean that?"

"I can't breathe," Zarina gasped.

She quickly let go. "Sorry."

Zarina put her hands on her narrow hips. "I've been evaluating my life lately, realizing what's important to me. My marriage for one—that silly crush I had on your friend was just lust. Pure, unadulterated, pulse-pounding lust. And two—family. So, about this psychic business . . ."

Anjali held her breath. Her sister had defended her, but would it be too much to hope she accepted her as well?

Zarina continued, "Are you free next Saturday? Vijay's mother wants to have you over. She wants to do a séance."

"Séance?"

"Please?"

Anjali looked at her sister's hopeful face and relented. "I'm free."

Zarina smiled. "Thank you. If you ever need a favor, just ask."

"There you girls are!" Mrs. Kumar moved toward them,

elbowing people out of her way. "What were they thinking having the party in such a small place? Cheapskates."

Anjali gasped. "Mom, they'll hear you."

"So what? I want to talk to you girls about something."

"Like?" Zarina said a tad nervously.

Their mother pointed to a group of older women. "Look at them. Do you know I'm the only one of them without a grandchild?"

Anjali tried to distract her. "Mom, did you read that horrible article about me—"

"I don't want to talk about ghosts. I want to talk about grandchildren." Her voice started to rise. "Will I even have one before I die?"

"Mom, people are listening," Zarina protested.

"God has blessed us with reproductive organs for a reason. Why not use them? You girls aren't getting any younger."

Anjali didn't think her mother would be satisfied until her offspring repopulated the entire planet. She decided to make a break for it. "Mom, this conversation doesn't really apply to me. I'm not even married. Zarina, on the other hand . . ."

Her sister's mouth fell open.

Their mother turned the full power of her maternal gaze on Zarina. "Is Vijay not virile enough? He does seem to be on the weak side."

Zarina's mouth was still open. A gurgling sound emanated from it.

Mrs. Kumar scanned the room with a sharp look. "Where is that Vijay? I want to talk to him. I think it's time the two of you came to Tempe. Everyone has grandchildren there. Such a happy place."

Anjali smiled at her sister. "Call us even. See you at the séance."

Humming to herself, she walked away.

53

"**I**'m sorry I missed your cousin's party," Coulter said from where he was sprawled on the sofa.

It was the following afternoon and they were all gathered in the firm's den.

"You're a famous man now," Anjali teased. "You had to meet with your agent."

"What exactly is an agent going to do for a psychic?" Eddie asked. As it turned out his leg wasn't broken, but he did have a very impressive row of stitches going up his shin.

"The man thinks I've got star quality," Coulter said lazily. "I believe he called me the love child of Matthew McConaughey and David Copperfield."

"Does he think you're humble too?" Scott asked.

"Have you heard anything about Vivica, Eddie?" Anjali asked.

"Well, the university disbanded the parapsychology department, as you know. So we're both out of a job."

"*Were* out of a job," Scott corrected.

Eddie grinned. "Where are those business cards you promised me anyway?"

"How much is Wilder paying you?" Coulter asked. "I bet there's a sweatshop in Chinatown that pays more."

"You were saying?" Scott said to Eddie. "About Vivica?"

"Apparently she's writing another book. Something about having survived a deadly psychic attack."

Everyone looked at Coulter.

He yawned and stretched. "All publicity is good publicity. If it isn't, I'll sue her."

"We're a team," Scott said. "You won't have to deal with her alone."

"That's beautiful, boss."

Scott ignored him. "And from a strictly business perspective, we're a success. There is no investigative firm like ours in the world. Powered by real psychics, solving those cases with a paranormal or supernatural bent."

Anjali looked puzzled. "I've been meaning to ask you. What's the difference anyway?"

"The supernatural relates to existence outside the natural world. While the paranormal deals with the range beyond normal experience or scientific explanation."

"I still don't get it," Coulter said. "Are ghosts paranormal, and angels and demons supernatural."

"Well, if angels and demons are supernatural, then ghosts should be too; they're all dead," Anjali pointed out.

"Technically, angels and demons are not dead. They're not even human," Eddie clarified.

"Wait," Anjali said. "How can an entity be paranormal when it's basically a demonic presence? And demons are supernatural, right?"

"The Devil is supernatural," Coulter explained, "But not demons. Am I right, boss?"

"So miracles and stuff like that is paranormal then," Anjali said.

Scott shook his head. "No, miracles are supernatural."

Coulter yawned again. "What's the difference between the supernatural and paranormal again? If I'm goin' to hell, I really oughta know."

Epilogue

Ensenada, Mexico

Three very pale men wearing Bermuda shorts, Hawaiian shirts, and sandals, sat around a small table littered with empty *Corona* beer bottles.

"I don't know how I let you guys talk me into this trip," Maddox said. "All we ever do is get drunk."

"That's cause beer is cheaper here," Fitch pointed out.

Gaspar rubbed his stomach. "Do you guys think I'm getting fat?"

"Let me see that clipping again," Maddox said.

Fitch pushed it across the table toward him. Maddox snatched it up and scanned the lines. "Do we really think the man the article refers to is Hans?"

"Come on," Gaspar said. "The guy was trapped in the

wreckage of his car. Gasoline is everywhere, an explosion is imminent and then a mystery man with eyes the color of fish scales comes out of nowhere and rips off the car door, drags the guy to safety, all without touching him?"

"It also says here that the guy in the car was half marinated in tequila at the time."

"You know I haven't had a drop of tequila since I've been here," Fitch said.

Maddox looked at him. "You had a margarita for breakfast."

"So?"

"What kind of alcohol do you think they use in—" Maddox shook his head. "Forget it."

"Look," Gaspar said. "It doesn't hurt to check out the story. And if we find Hans . . . well, you heard what the General at the DOD said. This could be very good for us."

"What do you think they'll do to him?" Fitch asked. "Do you think it'll be like that movie, *The Fury*? Those scientists performed experiments on Kirk Douglas's psychic son until his brain exploded."

Maddox stood and threw a few bills down on the table. "I'm going back to the hotel. I think I've got sunstroke."

Gaspar watched him go. "What's up with him?"

"Didn't you hear?" Fitch said. "He's got sunstroke."

"I'm going too. I want to talk to the guy Hans supposedly saved." He stood and threw down a few bills."

"Wait for me," Fitch said and pulled a few bills from his wallet, adding them to the stack on the table. He started after Gaspar, then turned back to the table, went through the pile of money and shoved half the notes back into his wallet. He took off.

Sitting quietly behind a newspaper nearby, a slight man with eyes the color of fish scales, slowly stood up, tucked the newspaper under his arm and sedately headed in the same direction Fitch and Gaspar had taken. He sang softly under his breath in a voice that was high-pitched and heavy at the same time, sexless. It wasn't a catchy tune.

Then again, Hans had always liked it.

Want More?

Turn the page to enter
Avon's Little Black Book —

the dish, the scoop and the
cherry on top from
SONIA SINGH

When I was thirteen, I encountered a ghost.

There weren't any rattling chains or bloodcurdling screams or speaking in tongues, but the experience was scary enough for me. Thank you very much.

The year was 1987, and my mother decided it was time for a visit to India.

I wasn't too keen on the idea. My last visit there three years before had resulted in a nasty stomach bug and traumatic nightly attacks from mosquitoes intent on my sweet American blood.

On the other hand, I did like the idea of ditching pre-algebra for three weeks.

It wasn't until our plane was somewhere over the Pacific Ocean that I learned all my teachers had sent a suitcase full of homework assignments to be completed during my trip abroad.

On the train journey from Delhi to Amritsar (the northern town where my grandparents lived and our final destination), we stopped off in Ludhiana (I kept calling it Louisiana) to visit my mother's cousin, Muna.

Muna lived in a small two-story house, and her daughter, Nithiya, was my age. The first thing Nithiya said to me, eyes narrowed behind her glasses, black braids reaching to her waist, was, "Everyone says America smells."

"India smells worse," I countered, and we both glared at each other.

Aunt Muna beamed at us. "I can tell you girls are becoming fast friends."

My mother agreed and therefore decided to leave me at her cousin's for two days while she and my eight-year-old brother, Samir, took the bus to visit some of my father's relatives.

I protested this decision but my arguments went unheeded. "You'll have more fun here," my mother said. "Muna is a wonderful cook and you can sleep in Nithiya's room. Besides, there is no indoor plumbing in your father's village, just the sugarcane field."

That first night at the dinner table as Muna and the family servant, Khaki, a cheerful woman in her thirties, served the meal, I thought the experience might not be too bad. The first dish I tasted—a cucumber, tomato, and red onion salad flavored with salt and cumin—was delicious.

"I wanted Chinese," Nithiya complained as her mother took a seat and Khaki returned to the kitchen to eat her own dinner.

"Tomorrow," Muna said.

Nithiya glared at me from across the table. "Chinese food tastes better in India."

"That's not true," I said. "I haven't seen a single Chinatown anywhere." (At thirteen this seemed like sound logic to me.)

She sneered. "We don't need a Chinatown. China is just across the border."

She did have a point.

Muna smiled at me. "You girls are just like your mother and me at that age. We were fast friends."

I wondered what the definition of "fast friends" was in India anyway. Maybe just knowing somebody made them a friend?

"Rakesh, have some more salad," Muna said.

I'd forgotten that my uncle Rakesh was there. He sat quietly, shoveling food into his mouth.

Muna picked up a piece of yogurt-marinated chicken and placed it on her plate. "Baba came to see me last night. He says we never should have painted the house."

Across from me, Nithiya slowly put down her glass of water and stared at her mother, eyes wide. Rakesh frowned and stopped eating.

I had no idea who this Baba person was and helped myself to a chicken breast.

That night, while I climbed into bed beside Nithiya and hoped those braids of hers wouldn't come near my pillow—the smell of coconut oil conditioner was overpowering—I found out who Baba was.

Babaji is my grandfather—Mama's father and your great-uncle."

"Oh."

Nithiya's glasses were sliding down her nose and she pushed them back up. "Don't you know anything? Babaji died five months ago and Mama keeps saying she sees him!"

"Oh . . ."

I felt a chill creep up my spine. "Have you seen . . . him?"

"No," she said and turned off the light.

I curled up on my side away from her and huddled under the covers. I didn't know what was more frightening. That Babaji's ghost was hanging around or that Aunt Muna was crazy.

The next morning my aunt claimed Baba had paid her another visit. "He wanted to know who you were," she said, looking at me. "I told him you're Manjeet's daughter. From California." She giggled. "He thought you were a boy."

Self-consciously, I touched my hair. A disastrous short cut a few weeks before had led to my being mistaken for a boy in America, India, and now the supernatural plane of existence.

I felt a sharp stab of homesickness. I wished my mom was there instead of squatting in some sugarcane field.

That afternoon we accompanied Aunt Muna on her errands. I was afraid we'd be traveling by rickshaw, but she loaded us into a cream-colored hatchback called a Maruti and we took off.

As the hatchback darted in and out of traffic, dodging mopeds, bullock-driven carts, and rickshaws, I kept my eyes trained on my aunt, but she appeared normal, cheerfully making Babaji-free conversation as we stopped by the tailor, the jeweler, and finally the stationer's so Nithiya could buy colored pencils. Last but not least, we pulled alongside a food stall, and Aunt Muna rolled down the window as a skinny barefoot man ran to the car to take her order. It took me a few seconds to realize we were at the Chinese restaurant.

From what I could see there wasn't a single Chinese person working the stall, just a large range covered with woks right there in the open. Stray dogs ran around in a circle, sniffing the air and barking.

I was hoping the egg rolls wouldn't taste like curry but

all my fears were dashed at dinner that evening when the food tasted like real Chinese takeout.

After dinner, Nithiya wanted to watch a movie showing on TV. Since I had nothing better to do, I joined her in the family room. It turned out the movie was *Annie* and it was dubbed in Hindi.

Nithiya scowled. "Why can't they leave it in English? I hate dubbed pictures."

I'd seen *Annie* a dozen times but it was kind of cool watching Daddy Warbucks yell in Hindi.

"Why did they name the bodyguard Punjab?" Nithiya demanded. "He's not Indian."

I shrugged. " I don't know. I never thought about it."

"Americans know nothing of our culture."

By the time the credits rolled across the screen it was almost eleven and we were both yawning. Nithiya turned off the TV and was about to switch off the light when the rocking chair in the corner creaked and began rocking.

I was sitting on the Persian rug covering the floor, and Nithiya stood near the floor lamp.

"That was his chair," she whispered. "Babaji?"

I was so scared, I couldn't move. From what I could tell, Nithiya wasn't too excited about a family reunion either.

For what seemed like ages but was probably five minutes, the chair continued to rock, and then without warning . . . it stopped.

That night we slept with the light on.

The next morning as Aunt Muna doled out omelets, I kept waiting for Nithiya to say something. She didn't. My aunt didn't bring up Babaji either.

When my mom and brother arrived, I practically flew to their side. I was so happy to see them that I didn't even mind when my mom made me do my pre-algebra homework on the train.

I did mind when my brother spilled buffalo milk all over it though.

The remainder of our visit was thankfully ghost-free.

Now, almost twenty years later, I'm positive that what I experienced that night—besides watching *Annie* in Hindi—was a visit from Nithiya's dead grandfather. To this day I've never seen a rocking chair start rocking on its own and then stop mid-rock minutes later.

My dad thinks it was probably the vibration from a moving train (the station was less than a mile from my aunt's house) or a tremor from a small earthquake. But I was sitting on the floor. Wouldn't I have felt any vibrations coming from the ground?

My mom believes me. According to her, India is crawling with ghosts. "If you offer them some candy and ask them nicely to leave, they usually listen. If not, a pundit will come to the house and blow cow-dung smoke."

I've taken her advice to heart. If a spirit ever does pay me a visit, I've got it covered. There's a drawer full of candy in the kitchen (which I don't touch, I swear). Now I just need a pundit to hook me up with some cow dung.

The smell should scare the dead, if not the living.

SONIA SINGH

Wen T. Chang

SONIA SINGH is the author of *Goddess for Hire* and *Bollywood Confidential*. She lives in Orange County, California. She is not psychic.